EVERYONE WANTS TO BE
AMBASSADOR TO FRANCE

EVERYONE WANTS TO BE AMBASSADOR TO FRANCE

◆ ◆ ◆

stories

BRYAN HURT

🐓 Red Hen Press | *Pasadena, CA*

Stories in this collection appeared in the following publications: *The American Reader, Connu, Denver Quarterly, Guernica, Hot Metal Bridge, Joyland, Kenyon Review, Los Angeles Review of Books, New England Review, Salt Hill Journal, Tikkun, Tin House, The Toast, TriQuarterly,* and *Watchlist: 32 Stories from Persons of Interest.*

Book design by Mark E. Cull

Library of Congress Cataloging-in-Publication Data
Names: Hurt, Bryan, author.
Title: Everyone wants to be ambassador to France / Bryan Hurt.
Description: Pasadena, California: Red Hen Press, [2018]
Identifiers: LCCN 2017052115 | ISBN 9781597097000 (softcover)
   eISBN 9781597097512
Classification: LCC PS3608.U779 A6 2018 | DDC 813/.6—dc23
LC record available at https://lccn.loc.gov/2017052115

The National Endowment for the Arts, the Los Angeles County Arts Commission, the Ahmanson Foundation, the Dwight Stuart Youth Fund, the Max Factor Family Foundation, the Pasadena Tournament of Roses Foundation, the Pasadena Arts & Culture Commission and the City of Pasadena Cultural Affairs Division, the City of Los Angeles Department of Cultural Affairs, the Audrey & Sydney Irmas Charitable Foundation, the Kinder Morgan Foundation, the Allergan Foundation, the Meta & George Rosenberg Foundation, the Riordan Foundation, and the Amazon Literary Partnership partially support Red Hen Press.

Second Edition
Published by Red Hen Press
www.redhen.org

For Marielle

CONTENTS

EVERYONE WANTS TO BE
AMBASSADOR TO FRANCE

THE BEAST OF MARRIAGE

Thomas Day was rich but very ugly. He couldn't dance. "Who will marry me?" said Thomas Day. He thrust his hands into his pockets and asked his friend Richard. Richard took out his snuff box, lit a pipe. "My sister will marry you," said Richard. But Richard's sister wouldn't marry him. Not even for all of his money, she said. Or all of the money in England, she said. He was that ugly. He was that bad at dance. "What about Anna Seward?" said Thomas Day. But Anna Seward heard about this and married someone else.

Thomas Day went to the orphanage and adopted two girls. The girls had names but he didn't like them. "From now on you will be Lucretia," he said. "Sabrina," he said. The girls were eleven and twelve years old. Thomas Day promised to make at least one of them into his perfect wife. He hired a boat and they all sailed to France.

But in France nobody had a good time. Thomas Day, it turned out, didn't like French people. He didn't like French roads. In a letter to Richard: "The women prefer their lapdogs to their children; the roads are full of holes." The girls got smallpox. They got fevers. They got mucus and pustules. Their crying kept him up all night. When they recovered they went on another boat ride, this time just for pleasure. The boat flipped over in the Rhône.

Eight months it went on like this. Thomas Day dueled a French person. Thomas Day dueled a French person. Thomas Day dueled a French person. Thomas Day hated dueling as much as he hated French people. But in France what could he do? Whenever he went to the coffeehouse or the market there was always another French person insulting him in French. The girls went to all the duels: duels by the river, duels in the field, duels at daybreak, duels at dusk. They'd sit on the ground and pull up grass.

And what about the girls? Turned out that Lucretia wasn't perfect wife material. "Perfectly stupid," Thomas Day wrote to Richard. When Thomas Day came back to England he apprenticed her to a milliner in Ludgate Hill. Later she married a linen draper. Everyone agrees that she lived a very happy life.

Thomas Day and Sabrina moved to Lichfield. Thomas Day rented a big house in the country. He invited Richard over, invited lots of other people as well. There were hors d'oeuvres and a string quartet. But when the people wanted to dance Thomas Day wouldn't let them. He took the bow from the violinist. No one was allowed to dance.

Everyone met Sabrina. They all agreed that she had long eyelashes for a thirteen-year-old and fine auburn hair that hung in ringlets on her neck. "I will teach her to become the perfect wife," said Thomas Day. "Bravo," said Richard. Then there was the toast.

But Sabrina wasn't the perfect wife. She failed all of the tests. The pistol test, for example, where Thomas Day fired pistols at the girl and told her not to move. The hot wax test, which was just like the pistol test but, instead of shooting pistols, dripping hot wax. Richard asked Thomas Day why he was shooting guns at the girl. "Stoicism," said Thomas Day. "My wife should be as fearless as the Roman heroines; she should be as intrepid as Spartan wives." "Are you firing real bullets?" asked Richard. They looked at the girl, trembling and crying on the ground.

Then Thomas Day fell in love with another girl. She wasn't a girl, technically, because she was the same age as Thomas Day. Her name was Honora Sneyd and she combined everything Thomas Day wanted in a woman. Fortitude of spirit, literary and scientific tastes, a disinterested desire to please. Thomas Day offered her his noble hand. She told Thomas Day that she'd think about it. Really, she'd think about it. Even though he was ugly. Even though he couldn't dance. Meanwhile, Thomas Day sent Sabrina to boarding school in Warwickshire. She was very happy there. Very happy. She was the happiest girl to have ever been sent away to boarding school. Her letters to Thomas Day went like this: "I'm so happy. Happy. Happy. Happy. Happy."

Honora Sneyd broke Thomas Day's heart. All women eventually broke Thomas Day's heart. Even his mother. She broke his heart by dying. He was one year old. Honora Sneyd broke Thomas Day's heart because she could not love him. She tried, she said. Her heart, she said, could not be schooled into softer sentiments in his favor. Thomas Day made a list of things that could not be schooled. The list went:

1. Hearts.
2. Girls.

Honora Sneyd broke Thomas Day's heart two more times. The second time when she married Richard. The third when she died.

There were other girls who broke his heart. Elizabeth Sneyd, for example, who was Honora's sister. She broke his heart by playing with it. Told Thomas Day that she could love him for his money, but only if he learned how to dance. But when he returned from Bath she changed her mind. She liked him better the other way. Before he could waltz, she said. Before he could dance minuets.

Later Thomas Day moved to London. He lived alone and wrote a poem about slavery and a book for children. Both were met by great success. He wrote letters to Sabrina at boarding school and, eventually, he wrote letters to Richard. Sabrina forgave him. He forgave Richard. In the letters everyone felt sorry about everything that had happened. At least they said they did.

And there were other things besides the girls. Like Thomas Day's love for horses. He liked to talk about the gratitude, generosity, and sensibility of horses. Whenever he met a disobedient or unruly horse he blamed its behavior on the mistreatment it must have suffered at the hands of its owner. He died trying to break a new horse. He was never a very good horseman, and the horse threw him off its saddle and stepped on his head. At the funeral everyone agreed that it was just like him to try to break a horse without a whip or a horsebreaker. "A victim of his own uncommon systems," said Anna Seward. Foolish, said everyone else, that he would shoot his guns at girls but that he tried breaking a horse with kindness instead.

HONEYMOON

1

The day before their honeymoon she got the flu. Then in the airplane she got an ear infection. In Paris the doctor gave her eardrops which gave her a skin rash because of her penicillin allergy. Then he got her flu and they got in a fight about the hotel because the walls were thin and they could hear the neighbors fucking. "Why not?" he said. "It's our honeymoon," he said. "We're sick," she said. "You're puking. Your head is in the toilet." Other than that it was a nice hotel. There was a toilet *and* a bidet *and* marble columns in the room *and* a receptionist named Laurent who brought them ice for her rash in a silver bucket at three in the morning. Eventually she got better and he got better and they left the hotel to go to museums. They looked at paintings and sculptures, some of which they'd seen before in their college textbooks. They saw some that they'd heard of but hadn't seen before and others that they'd never even heard of. "I didn't know Monet painted asparagus," she said. "It says Manet," he said, pointing at the nameplate.

There was a subway strike. It rained the entire time. They walked everywhere. They got blisters, got wet, got sick again. They got in another fight back at the hotel room. "You're not supposed to tip," he said. "But Laurent's been so nice," she said. "You're not *supposed* to," he said. "It's offensive. It's against their culture." They sat on the king bed and watched French-dubbed versions of American TV shows. Cop shows mostly but also sitcoms and soap operas. They made up and ordered champagne from Laurent even though their heads were sick and already fuzzy.

Still they did not have sex, no sex, not on their honeymoon. His flu became a sinus infection. Her skin rash continued spreading. They went to churches, the Eiffel Tower, more museums. They got bored, got into another fight about all of the fights they'd been getting into. "I'm not fighting," she said, "you're fighting." "You're fighting," he said. "You're the one who's fighting." He sat on the bed and she left the hotel room to go walking. "Walking," she said when he asked where she was going. "It's raining," he said. But maybe she hadn't heard him because of the hotel room door slamming.

2

They went to another hotel. This one in the south of France on an island. Used to be a shipbuilder's house is what the concierge told them. This concierge was also named Laurent but he had gold epaulets on his red jacket. "Wi-Fi?" he asked, our man, the honeymooner. "No Wi-Fi," said Laurent. He said that the shipbuilder's house had been built during the sixteenth century. And so the hotel had original sixteenth-century details. Four-poster beds, strapwork, authentic wallpaper. No TV, no Wi-Fi. But their room had views of the shipyard where the shipbuilder built his ships. Which of course was no longer a shipyard but now instead was a clam café. The island's best, Laurent said. So they ate clams, did not check their email.

"Sex?" she said after clams. Because the island was sunny and sun is good for moods and rashes. She felt warm and full and better. But no, no sex. He was still upset about the Internet. "Disconnected," he said. "How will we know?" he said. There were things he wanted to know about. For example: his cat back home. Their cat, technically. But more his than hers since he'd had it since college. How was the cat doing, was it happy? He could not know because he could not email the cat sitter. He also wanted to know more about the island. Like where to eat. But with no Internet there was no Yelp and so no recommendations. Were the clams he ate any good? Were the best clams he could have eaten? He could not know.

"I thought they were good," she said. But she had steamed clams, he had clam chowder. There was no parity, no ground for comparison. "Let's go for a walk," she said. "Clear our heads. Sea air. Sunshine." He did not like this idea. Walks were her solution for everything. If they were doing her thing, they weren't doing his thing. It was like she was winning. But he went with her anyway, walking. Because maybe they would walk by something, an Internet café, or something.

They walked through town, over cobblestones, past souvenir shops, tourists, under striped awnings. They did not walk past an Internet café, at least if they did he did not see it. What was French for Internet anyway? They walked out of town, through meadows of sea grass, along a rocky beach, past the salt farms. They watched the salt farmers harvest salt. Sweating and sunburnt, dragging long rakes across evaporation fields.

There was the salty breeze, the sun, hot sun. "I don't feel good," he said. "Your flu?" she said. "Your sinus infection?" "My stomach," he said. He was clutching his stomach. Then she noticed his lips, which were pale and swollen. "Are you okay?" she said. He was dizzy. "Dizzy," he said. The sound of rakes through salt was making him nauseous. "My eyes," he said. Because now his eyeballs were itching. "You should sit down," she said. "Sit down." She was guiding him to the bench on the side of the path, a stone bench that looked out over the sea, deep, deep blue and with seagulls bobbing. But then she wasn't. Rather she was guiding, pulling him, but he had stopped moving. "Get up," she said, tugging his arm which was suddenly limp, not arm-like. He was lying on the path, on his back, gasping. She knelt down beside him. His breath on her cheek. Shallow breathing.

3

The third Laurent was the nurse at the hospital. This Laurent had a broad, puffy face, wide eyes with bags under them, was balding. "Anaphylactic shock," he said, shaking his head. "Very serious." It was funny, so funny, the ways that bodies change and surprise you. All of his life he, our man, had been one way. Now on his honeymoon he was suddenly another. Married with a shellfish allergy, deathly allergic.

Also funny were all the Laurents in France. Who knew there were so many? He asked Laurent about this. A common name, Laurent? It was not common or uncommon, Laurent said. Just a name that some people gave their children. He checked the man's pulse and hooked him into a new bag of saline. Then she came back from the cafeteria with sandwiches. They were simple sandwiches, bread and cheese, cut into rectangles. "Thank you, Laurent," she said. Laurent grunted. She gave her husband his sandwich. They ate cheese sandwiches, held hands, listened to the machine beeps, the man's heartbeats, thought about how close they'd come to losing each other. For the first time on their honeymoon, the very first time, it felt, really, like they were married.

So sex, of course, finally. After he was discharged, their marriage finally consummated. Back at the shipbuilder's house in the four-poster bed. Not the shipbuilder's actual bed, not likely. But he liked to think so. That they were sleeping in the same bed that the man who built ships five hundred years ago had slept in. "France has such a deep history," he said, now post-coital and somewhat melancholy. The afternoon sunlight was a white square on their white sheets, moving slowly. "Rich history," she said. "Rich," he said, "because marred with tragedy. The Revolution. The First World War. The Second World War." "Not to mention Joan of Arc," she said. "Yes," he said. "Joan of Arc." He pushed his fingers through her hair. "It's the tragedy," he said, "that makes history rich. The sadness that enhances culture." "It brings people closer together," she said. They kissed, ordered room service from Laurent, champagne and strawberries. Then they rode bikes to the beach, sat in the sand, watched the sunset.

Later they would tell their friends at home in Cleveland how good it was, their honeymoon. "Good food," they'd say. "Good art, good beaches. Good memories, good everything. Nothing bad that lasted."

4

But something lasted. If not the honeymooners' bad memories then bad memories of them. Laurent's, for example. The third Laurent's, the nurse's. The man and woman were sticky, gummed to his memory. When smoking a smoke-break cigarette in the ambulance bay, the thought would come to him: the man, the one with the clam allergies. Or he would think: that woman and her sandwiches. These thoughts annoyed him. Sudden adult onset clam allergies were serious but not that uncommon, so why were his thoughts stuck on them, this man and that woman? He hadn't even liked them.

These were his thoughts on the night they'd been discharged. Thinking about them and wishing he wasn't thinking about them. His shift over and driving home past the salt farms. Salt pond after salt pond looping past his windows. Windows down because he liked to hear the breeze through the beachgrass. The ocean's reflection of the full moon out the window to his right, rippling. Another thing, he thought, was that his father had been a salt farmer. His brother was *still* a salt farmer. Not easy work, backbreaking. Skimming salt sludge from seawater, drying it, shoveling it into wheelbarrows. They got paid by weight, which wasn't much, considering. But sea salt sold in tiny, expensive vials in gift stores to tourists. So somebody made money, at least, the shopkeepers.

It wasn't that he *blamed* the honeymooners for his father's death. Skin cancer, all those years under the sun, his cells cooking. Laurent didn't draw a straight line between his father's cancer and their participation in the salt economy. That wouldn't have been fair. Not fair at all, but easy to do. But he *didn't* blame them. Associated them with it, perhaps. Made them accessories after the fact, accomplices. But that was not why he hated them. Not because they bought salt, ate clams, perpetuated everything that made island life so small and oppressive. His dislike was deeper than that, more primal. Something in the smug way they held hands, ate their cheese sandwiches, said "Thank you, Laurent." As if Laurent was not a proper name but something you called a servant.

They weren't special, not special nor better than anyone else, really. Laurent had been on a honeymoon, too, you know—Los Angeles. He'd photographed the stars of Hollywood Boulevard, went to Disneyland, saw the tar pits, the saber-toothed tigers and woolly mammoths. But not all of life is a honeymoon. Even then he knew that. While on his honeymoon he knew that life wasn't a honeymoon. He wouldn't even have said that his honeymoon had been a honeymoon. It was fun, a nice vacation, but it wasn't perfect. He and his wife weren't *perfect*.

It was late when he got home, after midnight. He'd stopped at a beach, put his feet in the water, smoked cigarettes. His wife was sleeping, but when he came into bed he woke her. "You smell like cigarettes," she said. "I was smoking," he said. "At least take a shower," she said. "I put on clean sheets this morning." He ejected himself from the bed, stripped out of his undershirt, boxers, stood under the water. When did it come to be like this? *This*. He was sure that they used to like each other, but now it seemed that at best they tolerated each other. More likely it was a mutual and low-grade resentment. Tonight it was his cigarettes. Tomorrow it would be something else that annoyed her, and also his cigarettes. He'd always been a smoker. This wasn't a surprise that he'd dropped on her suddenly, like SURPRISE. They used to smoke together. When they were younger, they'd go to house parties at beach houses, get a little drunk, and stand outside on the patio sharing a cigarette, house music thumping inside the house. Now she acted as if she were above it and blamed him because he was not. It wasn't his fault that he was still the same person she'd married. He was still himself. She was the one who was different.

He would have told her this, too, if he'd had the chance. But she'd fallen back asleep by the time he'd finished his shower, and he wasn't yet the kind of person to wake another person up just to make a point. He would have also liked to have told her about the honeymooners, the man with the clam allergy. She'd have liked that anecdote, found it funny, because she was in the clam business. Bought them from farmers and sold them to restaurants. "A classic middleman," she'd said all those years ago when they met at the house party, shared a cigarette, and explained their jobs to each other. His favorite kind of small talk because his job was easy, not abstract. A nurse never had to explain to anyone what a nurse was. "Not a middleman," he'd said, feeling drunk and overfunny. "A middle*clam*."

Maybe it was better that she was asleep and he couldn't tell her about the honeymooners. The thought of them holding hands still made his heart beat angrily, and inevitably the conversation would have turned

around and back toward their own lives. There was the question he needed to ask her. The *question*. A question about who she'd eaten lunch with
the other day when he'd ridden into town on an ambulance, an emergency call that wasn't really an emergency, a German tourist with sun-
stroke. If that was an emergency then it was a common emergency, one
that happened a dozen times a day. Still he was happy to get out of the
hospital, liked the EMTs because they told dirty jokes, liked the tourist
part of town because of the old buildings, a nice change of pace. While
the EMTs worked on the German, he stepped away from the ambulance
to smoke a cigarette. That's when he saw her sitting at a table with an
umbrella outside the clam café across from the hotel that had been the
shipbuilder's house. Not unusual because she often met there with clam
buyers. But unusual because the man she was meeting with was not a
clam buyer. A concierge by the looks of it, gold epaulets, red jacket. Obviously not a clam buyer because of the way she was leaning across the table,
holding hands, and under the table, the way she was rubbing her foot up
and down his leg.

Perhaps he was mistaken. Perhaps it wasn't his wife he had seen that
day but someone who looked extremely like her. It was possible. Anything
was possible, even on a small island, an island as small as this one. In the
morning he could ask her about it. He could ask her if he really wanted to
ask. The only thing that was impossible was un-asking. Once he asked he
could not take it back. And let's say he was mistaken. In marriage, accusing
your spouse of cheating on you is one thing you can't be mistaken about.

Laurent closed his eyes and tried to summon sleep. He was not happy
but he was not unhappy. What do you call that medium place between
one thing and another thing? It wasn't nothing. He was pretty sure that
what he felt was not a lack of affect. He felt something. He thought about
the honeymooners again. Maybe he was stuck on them because what he
felt was an uncomfortable kinship. They were also in a transitional state,
suspended between one thing and another thing. Nothing had changed
but everything was changing.

5

The first Laurent, the Laurent back in Paris, remembered the honeymooners, too, but more fondly. Sure they did not tip, but he could not help it, he liked them anyway. Ice for your rash? A bucket for your vomit? An umbrella because it's raining? It wasn't often that he felt so needed.

He felt melancholy when they left for the island, but it was a good island, and he knew they would be happy. "Goodbye," he said, "Au revoir," and loaded their bags into the trunk of the taxi, waving. Then he went back to work. He had a few more hours in his shift. He loaded more bags into taxis, helped a couple who had lost their passports. He didn't mind. He liked working.

After his shift he changed out of his hotel uniform, into civilian clothes. He walked along the banks of the river and admired the old bridges that crossed over it. The stonework, the rumble of the cars and footsteps above him. The river was turning pink and orange, the sun was setting. He loved his city. He loved his city because everyone loved it. He'd never lived anywhere else, could not imagine it.

After Pont Neuf, he turned away from the river. Stopped at a bar for a glass of white wine, listened to the chatter of the other bar patrons, and underneath that, strains of Mozart. He looked at his watch. By now the honeymooners' train would be arriving at the island. He hoped they liked it. He hadn't been there in many years but he remembered it as a quiet place, old and charming. He remembered bike rides, beachgrass, ice cream cones at sunset. How lucky, he thought. He'd been very lucky.

He finished his wine and walked through the narrow side streets, his head pleasantly buzzing. Yellow lights glowed on in the apartments above him. From the open windows, domestic sounds. TVs, pans clattering. He had never been married. He'd had lovers, sure, men mostly, but women too. He'd always believed in Eros, love as pure expression, not in the strictures of bodies, but he'd never found love that lasted. Inevitably love grew cold, he and his lover became distant, would end amicably.

He did not regret this except for sometimes when he came home from work, poured himself some of the morning's cold coffee, turned on the

TV, and shared his day with no one. Had it been only a month since he and his last lover had drifted? There was still evidence in the apartment that not so long ago his life had been very different. A comb, a toothbrush, a paperback that he himself would never have been caught dead reading. It was lonely. He could not deny that it was lonely. But even then it was not such a bad life. He watched the news people on the TV recount the day's tragedies: someone died, someone died, somewhere faraway many people were dying. He had his health, at least. He had friends, he had a job he found fulfilling. He thought about the honeymooners, their flu, their rash. They were lucky, they were young and had really never suffered. There was so much real suffering in front of them, so much sadness. You didn't have to watch it on TV, you only had to live life a little to know that it was full of unexpected sadness. This honeymoon of theirs, this time together, it was a gift, no matter how impermanent.

He cooked an omelette, had another glass of wine, watched the news become a soap opera. His phone rang and he let it ring a few times before answering. It was the hotel, the desk clerk, his nighttime counterpart. There was an emergency, the clerk said, an emergency. Something about a young couple and stolen passports. He said that Laurent was needed. *Needed.* What a rush. He would be there, Laurent said. He was lacing his shoes. He was on his way already.

THE BILINGUAL SCHOOL

So we sent our kids to the bilingual school. It was Mrs. Eagle's idea. She'd found it on her morning walk. Turned down Milwood Avenue instead of cutting across Crescent Court, looked up from her steaming cup of Starbucks, and there it was, a school inside a tall blue fence.

On the fence were bright paintings of charming and childish things: airplanes, flowers, tigers.

The sign above the doorway read: L'ÉCOLE BILINGUE, ENGLISH AND FRENCH.

All of this was written in a fancy white script.

Inside the fence she heard the happy sounds of children. She pressed her face to a knothole and saw children playing hopscotch. Children swinging the tetherball. Children clutching leather-strapped books and nodding smartly to each other. All of them in perfect black berets.

Across the street was the public school, the middle school where we would have to send our children when they got to be that age. Outside, there were children lazing on the steps. Children smoking cigarettes. Children practically fornicating with other children. At home Mrs. Eagle called the rest of us. A meeting for concerned parents, she said. Mothers who are concerned about the education of their children.

We ate madeleine cookies at the meeting. Dipped them in tea and talked about how exciting it would be for our children to learn French.

French is the language of love, said Mrs. Davis.

But not amorous love, I hope, said Mrs. Cavendish, who happened to be our host. She moved around the living room, pouring more tea.

No, said Mrs. Eagle. Italian is the language of amorous love. Spanish is the language of forbidden love. German is the language of modern love. English is the language of self love. French, she said, is the language of brotherly love.

We all agreed that brotherly love was the best.

Then Mrs. Spatz took out a picture book and we looked at pictures of French couples carrying umbrellas. French couples eating croissants. French couples riding tandem bicycles along the green banks of the Seine. Mrs. Spatz began humming "Aux Champs Elysées."

At first our kids didn't want to go to the bilingual school. They wanted to know what was wrong with their current school. What was wrong with primary language–only education?

We explained that their current school was failing them. Primary language–only education was making them vulgar and limited in expression.

Mrs. Cavendish had shown us a drawing her daughter had made in art class. It looked like an ill-formed dog hopping over a fence.

A nice dog, said Mrs. Eagle.

It's supposed to be a horse, said Mrs. Cavendish.

We told our children that at the bilingual school they would learn to draw horses that looked like horses.

But they complained about the dress code. We don't like berets, they said. They're too hot in the summer, they said, and don't cover your ears in the winter.

We told them they should consider themselves lucky to wear berets.

We showed them pictures of famous beret wearers: artists, intellectuals, and Che Guevara.

Che Guevara is un-American, they said.

French is un-American, they said.

We admit they almost had us there for a moment. How had that picture of Che Guevara gotten in there?

We asked Mrs. Spatz, who was in charge of assembling the pictures. I think he's cute, she said.

We agreed that Che Guevara was cute. We liked his eyes and his cheek-bones. The rakish way he pursed his lips.

Che Guevara is cute, we told our children.

Berets are cute, we said.

French is cute.

There's nothing more American than being cute.

The children weren't the only ones to object to the bilingual school. Our husbands complained as well. They didn't understand why we should send our children to a special school. Didn't regular schools still teach French? We explained that bilingual schools didn't just teach the language. They taught culture, music, food, art.

Public schools can't teach you to listen to Debussy, we said.

Public schools can't teach you to appreciate soft cheese.

Over breakfast our husbands grumbled and looked at the brochures. There were turtle-necked children smiling happily on the covers. The Eiffel Tower towering in the background.

The costs, our husbands said.

The social stigma, they said.

They pointed out that the bilingual school didn't even have an American-style football team. Without American football how would our children learn to interact with their peers?

We cleared their breakfast plates and rinsed them in our sinks. We watched oily swells of bacon fat pool and cloud in the dishwater like our dreams.

What to do? we asked ourselves.

We gazed at pictures of Che Guevara. Asked ourselves: What would Che Guevara do?

Withhold sex, said Mrs. Eagle.

We were sipping Frappuccinos. We sat beneath an umbrella and shield-ed our eyes from the sun.

Mrs. Eagle explained that we would withhold sex until our husbands came to see our point of view. Mrs. Davis fanned herself with a napkin.

How long? she asked.

Until our request can no longer be denied, said Mrs. Eagle.

How long will that be? asked Mrs. Davis.

About a week, said Mrs. Eagle.

Mrs. Cavendish plunged her green straw into a plastic cup. What if we're already withholding sex? she said.

Mrs. Spatz removed her sunglasses. You have to have sex, she said, in order to withhold sex.

About a week later we sent our children to the bilingual school.

We walked them to the blue fence and said goodbye underneath a picture of a smiling tiger.

Goodbye, said our children.

And they were quickly assimilated into the playground by their peers, their black berets indistinguishable from all the others.

At the end of the day we met our children outside the blue fence.

Hello, we said.

Bonjour, they said.

Mrs. Eagle squealed with delight.

It went on this way for several weeks. We said goodbye outside the fence and they said au revoir. We said hello and they said bonjour.

They added other expressions to their vocabulary, such as s'il vous plaît, excusez-moi, and merci beaucoup. When we went to In-N-Out they ordered their cheeseburgers with pommes frites.

Even our husbands seemed impressed. How do you say American football? they asked.

Football, said our children.

How do you say soccer? said our husbands.

Football, said our children.

Our husbands smiled and shook their heads. They marveled at the ambiguity.

How do you say cows? said our husbands.

We were picnicking in the mountains. Picnic baskets on picnic blankets on the ground. Around us, cows were chewing grass.

Les vaches, said our children.

Our husbands continued asking.

How do you say chewing? How do you say grass?

While they asked, we women ate sandwiches. We removed them from our picnic baskets, unwrapped them, spread them with cheese. Mrs. Spatz said that cheese is a product of aging. Controlled spoilage, she said. Her twins taught her that. At the bilingual school they learned that cheese is created by souring milk, letting bacteria colonies settle and grow.

The smell of cheese is the smell of decay, she said.

We sniffed our sandwiches. They seemed to smell fine.

Mrs. Davis told us that her cheese smelled like soil.

Mrs. Eagle said that her cheese smelled like shoes. But good shoes, she said. Expensive. She took a bite.

Mrs. Cavendish said that the ability to ignore signs of death is a mark of civilization. By learning about cheese, she said, our children are learning to be civilized.

Cowbells clanked around us.

Our husbands and children, playing soccer, cheered.

Mrs. Davis was the first to notice that something was wrong. After school, her children continued speaking French. They'd sit at the dinner table and talk to each other in sentences that chimed like bells.

When she told them to brush their teeth they'd look at her, say something tinkling, and laugh.

When she asked them to take out the garbage they'd stare at her blankly, at the two Hefty bags in her hands.

Je ne sais pas, said the boy.

His sister: Je ne comprends pas.

And my husband is worthless, said Mrs. Davis. He just laughs. He thinks it's funny that they talk to us that way.

We were at Mrs. Cavendish's. Pictures of horses that looked like horses hung on her fridge.

What are they saying? asked Mrs. Spatz. She blew on her tea.

Exactly, said Mrs. Davis. It's impossible to know.

Mrs. Eagle said that it was very difficult to learn a foreign language without immersing yourself in it. They're immersing, she said.

But at home, Mrs. Eagle found her son sunning himself by the pool. His black beret seemed blacker. The felted wool soaking up all the light.

Bonjour, he said. His words chimed across the water.

Comment allez-vous?

Later that week we sat by the same pool. Suntan lotion wafted in the air. How old is he? asked Mrs. Davis.

Mrs. Eagle rolled onto her stomach. Ten, she said.

For tanning, said Mrs. Davis, ten seems kind of young.

Mrs. Spatz told us that her twins had suddenly become interested in mime. They actually do a great routine, she said. One blows up a balloon and hands it to the other. The other floats away. But they get paint everywhere, she said. Not to mention bedtime, she said. Whenever it's bedtime they become trapped in some kind of box.

We asked Mrs. Cavendish about her daughter.

Mrs. Cavendish leaned forward in her chaise. She's been teaching my husband, said Mrs. Cavendish.

Teaching him what? we said.

She's teaching him French.

For example, when they drove to Whole Foods. Mrs. Cavendish's husband would roll down the windows. Quel temps fait-il? he'd say.

Her daughter would stick her hand outside. Il fait bon.

Or at the movies: Qu'est-ce que j'ai raté? her husband would say.

Un tremblement de terre.

What'd you say? said Mrs. Cavendish. The audience hissed, someone kicked her seat.

Language is a fortress, she told us by the pool.

We knew exactly what she meant. Language is a fortress on St. Helena, we said.

Because when we said goodbye outside the bilingual school, we noticed that the children's au revoirs sounded less like goodbyes dressed up in a different language and more like actual goodbyes.

When we picked them up after school, we noticed how they lingered on the playground with their classmates, talking.

What were they saying to each other?

Each consonant, each nasally vowel, was building a wall between us. Brick by brique par brique.

We asked our husbands if they noticed anything going on. But they were husbands. They gazed into their smart phones, playing Threes! and Angry Birds, said no.

Then there was the strike, and the strike was impossible to ignore.

We don't know why it started exactly. Mrs. Davis told us her children weren't doing their homework.

Homework? we said.

We hadn't seen our children doing homework either.

We asked them about it.

They flipped TV channels: top models, top chefs, got talent.

How do you say? they said. En grève, they said.

We knew what en grève meant. We're not the types of mothers who don't watch the evening news. We'd seen the marches in Lyon and Paris. The marchers with en grève banners. Hand-painted. Red paint.

And what are you striking about? we asked. But the children wouldn't say anything more about it.

En grève, they said. They continued flipping channels, berets perched defiantly on top of their heads.

We met with the headmaster. We waited outside his office and pulled our skirts closer to our ankles. We crossed our legs and then crossed them again. We coughed.

The inside of the bilingual school was just like the outside. Bright-colored walls with bright pictures of cheerful things.

Mrs. Spatz sat underneath a scooter.

Mrs. Cavendish sat underneath an apple.

Mrs. Davis sat underneath an ostrich.

Mrs. Eagle sat underneath an Arc de Triomphe.

The headmaster served us macaroons. He took off his beret and scratched his mustache. Told us he understood our concerns.

Mademoiselles, he said, everything is okay. How do you say? he said. Vos enfants grandissent. Your children are just growing up.

And maybe he was right. When we were children hadn't we done the same sort of things? Not strikes, exactly, but other things. Revolutions. Black nail polish. Che Guevara T-shirts. Punk.

I don't like it, said Mrs. Cavendish.

We agreed. We did not like it.

The headmaster shrugged: What's for you to like or not to like? Your children are condemned to be free.

That night, the bilingual school held an open house. The students presented on the difference between French and American education. The Davis siblings made existentialist dioramas. There was a baking contest and Mrs. Cavendish's daughter won for her éclairs. The open house ended with a mime skit led by the Spatz twins. At the end of their routine, they called all of the children on stage and blew up balloons for them. They all floated away.

In the summer we sent the children to France as part of a foreign exchange. They mailed us postcards of ducks on the Seine, shoppers on the Champs Elysées. Having a great time, they wrote. And scrawled as an afterthought: Wish you were here.

And a year after that they graduated from the bilingual school. There was a bilingual middle school, but we sent them to the public school. By then they didn't care about French or bilingual education. They cared about lazing around and smoking cigarettes and fornication. They didn't care about us.

It was hard at first, but eventually we were okay with that. It's not like we didn't care about them, but maybe we *didn't*, at least a little bit. We didn't care in the same ways we used to. After all, they didn't want us to walk them to school. They didn't want us to hold their hands. They didn't say anything when we wished them goodbye.

Sometimes when we saw them walking toward us, out of the middle school or into our houses, with their skinny jeans, with their longboards, their acne, greasy hair, they didn't even look like our children anymore. They seemed more like bad translations of our children.

Familiar but foreign concepts.

Half-unknowable.

Our children partially dubbed.

SEAGULL

In my town there was once a seagull who had been reincarnated as a man. But instead of forgetting he was a seagull and knowing that he was a man, the seagull knew from the moment he knew anything that he was and had always been a seagull. When he closed his man-eyes, he felt the rush of air through his tail feathers, smelled sea water, and could hear fish flip fins in the dark below. But when he opened his eyes, he'd see the cage bars of his crib, the sky trapped behind windows, birds free and winging away. Here he was lumpy and blubbering and soft-mouthed, without a beak.

The seagull's parents were kind but didn't understand. Raw fish? No way. We sleep in beds not nests of twigs and spit. Don't poop from that tree.

And at school no one understood him either.

The teachers: get away from that window. Sit down because we're serious about that window. Butt in the chair. But how he envied the housefly chasing the sky and sunlight, bumping against the warm pane.

And the students: pinning him to the playground woodchips, dangling the worm in front of his face. Eat the worm, bird. He would eat it but they were only half right. Seagulls were a suborder of the class Aves, in the family Laridae. Yes, he ate small animals and invertebrates, but he would have preferred something briny, a silver minnow or hard-shelled clam.

One day in middle school math, the seagull met a goat who had been reincarnated as a girl. It was around that time that we were beginning to suspect that the reincarnation system was glitchy, on the blink. Souls were being recycled but not scrubbed clean of old identities. Not just goats as girls and birds as boys but humans as dishwashers; my great-grandmother had come back as the engine of my parents' old Volvo, which was just like her, the constant knocking an old person's insistence on not being ignored.

The goat was chewing on the tab of a soda can when the seagull sat down beside her. At first she didn't pay attention to him but soon the teasing he attracted was impossible to ignore.

"Leave him alone," she said and wiped a spit wad off her neck. She glared at me specifically. I unhitched my arm and put the pink eraser back on my desk.

I did not dislike the seagull. We were neighbors and in elementary school and before that had even been friends. We'd climbed trees together, hunted for shiny objects, fished for minnows in the stream behind my house. But you know how it is in middle school. Stop acting like everyone else for a minute and they turn on you; suddenly you're the one who stands out.

Goats are social animals and quick to make friends. After math class, she and the seagull were inseparable. Every lunch they'd sit together in the cafeteria, near the marching band kids but separate, part of their own reincarnated clique. They'd talk about their lives before this one, ponder the karmic equation, wonder what they had done to deserve humanity: the worst. The goat unwrapped her sandwich and chewed the paper. She recalled her fine, soft goat coat, talked about a tasty hedgerow, a country house, a friendly dog tied to a rope. The seagull remembered flying in formation with other seagulls, sleeping in the warm ocean, a red and white lighthouse on a hill.

I sat alone at my table and pondered my own animal past life. I must have been a menace to others, something fierce and unrepentant, a rabies carrier, I was sure. Because in this life I had been reincarnated as the next lowest creature in all of middle school after the seagull, the lowest now that he'd allied himself with the goat.

A Cheetos wrapper bounced off my head. I picked it up, tallied my old sneakers and out-of-fashion backpack. A human with the soul of a honey badger, I told myself, reassuring. I walked my tray to the conveyor, dropped the wrapper on the goat's table for her to eat. The next day in math class she remembered my name, said Hi Ben, and made circles with her compass on graph paper, the line crossing lines and bending infinitely into itself.

I wasn't an official member of their clique but they let me hang out with them. After school, we'd stand along the brick wall waiting for busses. The seagull wasn't much of a talker, especially with me there, third-wheeling. He'd hop nervously in place while the goat and I chatted. I liked to talk about my old great-grandmother, the Volvo engine, still knocking. Recently my father had taken the car to a mechanic who of course found nothing. Now the knocking had become louder, a metallic clanking that you could hear halfway down the block.

The goat said she could understand this. Her parents were divorcing and she'd taken to wearing a brass bell around the house so that they'd hear her and stop fighting when she was about to enter a room.

When the busses arrived, the goat got on hers and the seagull and I got on another. The seagull always pushed on ahead of me; he'd find an empty bench, slide to the window, and leave an aisle seat open, an invitation that I'd never accept. If school was a wilderness, then the bus the wilderness's jungle. The seagull, animal-souled, should have known this better than anyone. No rules applied here except for the most basic one: survival. Together we would have only made ourselves bigger targets. Without the goat, who was taller than most, with broader shoulders, there was no strength in our numbers.

One day before we got onto our separate busses, the goat handed me a note. She told me not to show it to the seagull. "Don't show the seagull," she said. I nodded, unfolded the note, read it, and then followed the seagull onto the bus. He'd found his empty bench, slid to the window. I sat down next to him. He looked at me, surprised and grateful. But what can I say? I wasn't doing it for my own good conscience. It was extra hot that day, mid-summer transubstantiating into late October. The bus was full; all of the seats but two were taken. The other was next to a kid who'd been able to grow a full, dark beard since fifth grade. You could smell his hormones halfway down the aisle.

"What's that?" the seagull said. Keen-eyed he was peering at the note, trying to read inside the fold.

"It's nothing," I said.

"It's from the goat?" he said. He recognized her loopy handwriting.

I tried to shove the note inside my backpack but by then it was too late. The seagull's attention had drawn even more attention. The note was yanked out of my hands, into the air, and passed along the aisle until it stopped at the beard, who opened it, scanned it with his dim eyes, and bellowed:

"Ben's got a girlfriend. Ben's in love with the goat girl."

He poked his finger through the paper and began jerking the hole.

I cannot deny that there was some truth in what he was saying. The goat had asked me to the Harvest Dance, but we were not dating. Not boyfriend and goat-girlfriend yet. As for what he'd said about love: Who knew about love, especially in middle school? All I knew was the heat in my face whenever I thought about the goat girl, her long limbs and blonde ponytail. The way that my heart was beating.

The beard tore the note to pieces and the pieces were torn into smaller pieces that rained down on me and the seagull, confetti.

When the bus stopped the seagull got up and pushed into the aisle. This was the first stop; ours was the last one at the end of the line near the river. The seagull paused at the door, looked back at me with a long sad look that said cruel world, cruel world, and exited. The seagull wasn't in school the next day or the rest of the week after that. On Friday, the goat and I went to the Harvest Dance. There were haystacks, pumpkins, red punch, bluegrass. At the end of the dance she led me outside the gymnasium and let me put my hands up her shirt. Her girl breasts were small and warm. My hands were quivering. We stood like that for a while, underneath the bleachers, in the moonlight and shadows, a dozen other couples all around us, all of us getting felt up or feeling.

The seagull wasn't in school on Monday of the next week either. The goat and I sat side by side in math class, holding hands. The teacher droned on about triangles, the goat snapped her gum, and I doodled on a piece of paper. In my doodles the goat was a gold-caped superhero and I was tied to the railroad tracks, train coming. She'd swoop down in the nick of time and fly me away to her secret headquarters, where she'd recognize my true animal past self. Then we'd fight crime, Goat Girl and non-human Ben, together forever.

While I was doodling my phone buzzed, a text from my mother. HAVE U SEEN GREG?

Greg was the seagull's human name. According to my mother, no one had seen him since Sunday. He'd eaten dinner, complained about hay fever, went to bed early. When the seagull's mother came into his room the next morning she found his still-made bed, its pillows emptied of all their feathers.

I texted that I hadn't seen him in a week, but even so I had a good idea where he was. When the seagull and I were little we used to play on a high cliff overlooking the river, a scrap of land with a wind-stripped tree that jutted out above the water. Sometimes, and for reasons that I couldn't then understand, the seagull would grow quiet, sullen, close all of the doors and windows that opened into himself, like a house shuttering for winter. He'd stand on the edge of the cliff, look down at the river, the rocks, and out at the faraway horizon.

When the goat and I arrived that's exactly where we found him. We got out of the cab and saw the seagull standing on the edge of the cliff, arms spread and the sleeves of his gray sweatshirt sewn white and rippling with pillow feathers. We called his name but our voices were lost in the wind and the taxi's engine. It was a blue day and the sky was high and clear and the horizon so far away that you could almost believe that there was more than just this: this town, this school, these bodies, our puny, recycled lives. Where the river met the horizon you could almost see the gleam of the tall buildings of the city that sat next to the ocean. Eight million souls and how many of them were former animals? I imagined a whole feral community.

The seagull turned to face us as the goat and I got closer. "Stay back," he said. "Don't try to stop me." His eyes were red, his nose was running.

"Stop you?" I said. "Stop what?" I might as well have asked what color the sky was, or if grass died in the winter. It was all so painfully obvious.

"It's awful," said the seagull. "Awful. Every day I wake up and I'm like this. I'm a seagull." He flapped his arms, shedding feathers. "I thought you were my friends," he said. "But now, not even."

"I'm sorry," I said. There was a knife in my stomach. "I'll leave," I said. "It's my fault. You can have the goat back. That's the way it's supposed to be. Goat and seagull together."

"I don't want the goat," he said. "You don't understand. I don't want anything. I'm not even supposed to be here." His hands were fists now. His entire body trembling.

The whole time the goat was still and silent. Her eyes were soft and trained on something far away, something beyond the gleam of the city and the horizon. "You should do it," she said.

"What?" I said. I stepped away from her. "You're joking."

"Not at all," she said. "The seagull's right. We're not supposed to be like this. Not him, not me. Something's broken. If he jumps maybe he gets to reset, start over."

In the distance I heard a familiar metal clanking sound, my great-grand-mother the Volvo engine. I'd told my parents where I thought the seagull would be and they were on their way, probably with the seagull's parents, winding up the road to the top of the cliff, staging a rescue.

"Are you sure?" said the seagull.

The goat nodded. "You're a seagull," she said. "You'll always be a seagull. Do you think it will ever get any better?"

I wanted to protest. I wanted to say that of course it would get better. Didn't everything always get better? But I also understood that I wasn't one of them. I was just a human-souled human.

"What do you think?" the seagull said. He was looking at me. He'd stopped crying.

The wind had whipped up, ripping leaves off the lone tree. The clank-ing was getting louder. "I don't know," I said. "I mean, what if the system's so broken that you don't come back at all? What if all that's next is nothing? Isn't something, even a bad something, better than nothing?"

But the seagull wasn't listening. As I spoke he was scooting backward, heels on the edge of the cliff. He looked at the goat. "Will you come with me?"

The goat shook her head. "It's not so bad for me here," she said. "As a goat I was already half-domestic."

The seagull nodded. His feet were halfway off the cliff. A strong wind would have blown him over. "Tell my parents it's not their fault," he said. He stepped off the cliff. There was nothing. Just empty blue sky where the seagull had been standing, and then a small poof of feathers.

My parents' Volvo crested the hill. They parked and ran to us, my parents and the seagull's parents. "Greg?" they said. "Where's Greg?" His mother knew, was collapsing.

"He," I said. "I," I said.

It seemed so unreal, so unfathomable. I couldn't say anything.

The goat stood at the edge of the cliff and stared over the water. "Did you see?" she said. "He changed," she said. She said that after the seagull had stepped off the cliff a real seagull, a bird, had soared up and toward the ocean. They searched the river from here to the city and on the third day found the body.

The goat and I kept seeing each other for a month after that. I touched her breasts two more times and once she put her hand down my pants, gave me a hand job. Her parents divorced and the goat moved to another town with her mother, further up the river. We emailed for a while, sent pictures, text messages. Then we stopped, which was a relief because every time we talked, texted, or touched I was reminded of the seagull. I didn't blame the goat for what had happened even though she played a role. I played a role too. But I'm certain that he would have gone through with it, even if we hadn't been there and encouraged him. What I couldn't forgive her for was the lie she'd told about the seagull transforming and flying toward the ocean. A selfish and cruel thing to say, especially in front of his parents.

His parents were devastated, of course. They sold their house quickly and for a loss, moved away to a remote nowhere.

After what happened, the bullies in middle school left me alone. The beard and the rest of them found someone less tragic to pick on. I graduated middle school and went to a bigger high school where I was just a quiet kid, part of the scenery. Eventually my great-grandmother, the Volvo engine, stopped knocking. One muddy spring morning, my father turned the key in the ignition and nothing happened. A click. The engine wouldn't turn over.

When I graduated high school, I moved to the big city. I was still looking for that feral community and had rented a studio apartment above a foul-smelling noodle shop in the Village. But by the time I got there, everything had changed again. All of the humans I met had human souls and if they didn't, if they'd been animals in their past lives, most of them had jobs and families and had forgotten. Even the goat girl. We're friends on Facebook. She lives in the Midwest and has two blonde and long-limbed children.

The other thing I don't like about the city is that there's no sky here. Sometimes I look up and expect to see open, untethered horizon, but instead can only see blue and clouds caught in sides of buildings. Sometimes there are birds in the buildings too. Seagulls because the ocean is close by even though I never go there. But I can't tell if they're real birds or just reflections, or if they're flying toward the city or leaving.

MY OTHER CAR DRIVES ITSELF

In the nineteenth century, when Karl Benz pitched his car idea to investors, he tried to temper their expectations by telling them that demand would be limited because of lack of chauffeurs.

During the 1939 World's Fair, General Motors predicted that cars would be driving themselves in twenty years.

My point is that for almost as long as we've been imagining cars, we've been imagining that someone else would be driving them.

We are Google's chase team.

What we're chasing now is the red Prius that's approximately thirty feet in front of us. The Prius planes and curves on the California 1 as adroitly as any NASCAR. Around even the most rollercoaster-like turns, its speed is a steady thirty-five. Our van hurtles and weaves behind it, hugging the cliffs of Big Sur. More than four hundred feet below, waves break and churn against some very sharp rocks.

It's Monday, midday, and the sky is set with tiny white clouds. Somewhere near Bixby Bridge, Levandowski points out the window, excitedly, at what he says is a whale. He tells us that its tail just breached the surface of the water and disappeared. He presses the binoculars to his chubby face and continues scanning.

Clarke and I refuse to look. Clarke's behind the steering wheel. His knuckles are whiter than the clouds above and you can see the muscles in his jaw tense with concentration.

Levandowski points out the window again. "There it is," he says.

This time we look. Clarke looks and I look.

Down in the bay, there's a big spray of water, a black hump, and then the van's wheels are crunching over gravel. Clarke slams the brakes but still we're slung into the guardrail. Clarke starts yelling at Levandowski. I lift my laptop to make sure my pants aren't damp.

A few minutes later we're back on the road. Levandowski's sulking because Clarke threw his binoculars out the window. The Prius is gone.

I log onto Google Maps and see that the blue dot that signifies "Prius" has stopped moving. When we catch up, we see that the car has driven itself into a cliff. The front end's crumpled. There's smoke pouring out the engine. The LIDAR mast, with its forty-two lasers and tens of thousands of dollars worth of navigation equipment, has snapped off the roof and is scattered across the road.

Levandowski puts on his gloves and starts collecting the technology. Clarke looks like he's going to cry. I open the laptop and begin typing the incident report. The gist of which is:

We are fucked.

Next morning we're called into Page's office. That's Larry Page, as in Google's multibillionaire cofounder and CEO. He's read my report and basically agrees with its assessment:

Totally fucked.

He digs into his pocket and pulls out his cell phone, which he tosses onto the desk and asks what we think it is.

What I think is that it's exactly like that part in *Star Wars* where, during the Battle of Endor, Admiral Ackbar yells, "It's a trap!"

Because obviously.

Page clears his throat.

Clarke finds a stain on his tie and begins rubbing the hell out of it. Levandowski focuses on a spot on the wall, just above Page's head, and stares really hard. I slump in my chair. "It's a cell phone," I say.

"What?" says Page.

"Cell phone," I say louder.

"Wrong." Page picks up the cell phone and hurls it at us. It whizzes over our heads and explodes against the wall.

What that was, says Page, was a *smart* phone. And in terms of functionality, he says, it makes his Ferrari look like a retarded piece of shit.

Why, he wants to know, can't we make a car that's at least as smart as his smart phone?

Clarke looks at Levandowski.

Levandowski looks at me.

I look at my shoes.

Levandowski sighs.

"There was a whale," he says, and stops.

"It won't happen again," he says.

Page doesn't say anything. He picks up a stapler and begins squeezing. As we hurry out of his office, the stapler flies into the hallway and dents the wall.

Levandowski and Clarke want to go down to the lab to do another postmortem on the LIDAR. I tell them that I'm going to lunch. It's not even ten o'clock.

"Whatever," says Clarke. "Don't be evil," he says.

Google's motto used to be something we took seriously, but now it's something we say instead of saying something else.

"Don't be evil," I say back.

But instead of the commissary, I go to the parking lot and call Julia. Julia's a graduate student at Stanford.

I'm sleeping with her.

She's not my wife.

Julia and I met when we were demoing an early version of the Google Car. Both of us were in the Prius's backseat, letting it drive us around Stanford's campus. I was looking out the window. There were old brick buildings, green trees, the California sky.

It took me a while to realize that Julia was looking at me.

She was smiling.

"Things are in the saddle," she said, "and ride mankind."

She told me that that was Emerson. "'Ode, Inscribed to William H. Channing,'" she said. When we got back to her apartment, she told me that she was getting her doctorate in literature. She was writing a dissertation about representations of machines in poetry.

"Consilience" is what she wants to call her book. She says that it doesn't matter that the title's already taken. In fact, she says that's kind of the point.

Julia doesn't answer. I hang up before the phone goes to voicemail.

Instead, I press the icon on my phone that dials Tracy's number. Tracy who *is* my wife. Even before the phone starts ringing, I know that she's going to pick up.

Ten months ago she went on maternity leave and she hasn't gone off. Whenever we talk about her going back to work because, you know, we're making half of what we used to make, and so hard times, we end up getting in a big fight.

"Hello," she says, and I hang up.

I'm in the car and halfway to Stanford before I realize that she's calling me back.

When I knock on her office door, Julia looks up from her desk, first surprised and then disappointed.

"Oh," she says. "It's you," she says.

There's a catastrophe of papers spread out in front of her. She's wearing these reading glasses that magnify her eyes.

I ask whom was she expecting.

She scans the hallway and closes the door. "These *are* my office hours," she says. She asks what I want.

What I want, I tell her, is to take her to lunch.

She looks at the clock.

"Brunch?" I say.

We go to her apartment. It's a one-bedroom in Pacific Heights. Out the window, you can almost see the Golden Gate Bridge.

"You're sad," says Julia. She's holding my penis but she's essentially right. What I feel most of the time is something like sadness.

My wife has noticed it too. "Do we make you unhappy?" Tracy says sometimes after we've put the baby to bed. "Do you realize you frown all the time?"

I tell Julia that we lost a car.

"Another one?"

She sounds truly disappointed. But then she really believes in the project. When we first met I gave her the investor's pitch, the one that made them go nuts and give us all their money.

In America there are forty thousand automobile deaths per year. Ninety-three percent of those are caused by human error.

Every ten years that's the population of Oakland gone, in twisted metal and burning rubber, just like *that*.

At Google it's our conclusion that, when it comes to being drivers, people basically suck. The Google Car is our hands-on-our-hearts attempt to do something good.

The truth is that we're developing the Google Car because the technology's ripe. In ten years, autonomous driving is going to be the industry standard. Every car company, and most of the tech ones, has something in R&D. Drive around Silicon Valley for long enough and it'll begin to seem like every third car is being chased by a black van.

Back at the lab, Levandowski and Clarke are yelling at each other.

It turns out that in a very technical sense there was no accident. The Prius crashed because it was supposed to crash.

Telemetrics show that something small, perhaps a small animal, ran into the road in front of it. Once the LIDAR picked it up, the car swerved, which is exactly what it's supposed to do.

The question that Levandowski and Clarke are now debating is whether or not swerving is a good design feature.

Like is it better if the car swerves and crashes? Or if it continues plowing forward regardless of what's in its way?

Levandowski has a big heart so, of course, votes for swerving. He wants to know what happens next time when it's a kid or someone's dog.

"Don't be ridiculous," says Clarke.

Clarke says that Levandowski's argument is stupid. He says we can adjust the LIDAR so that it picks up bigger things like dogs and children.

The real question, he says, is if we're going to let an eighty-thousand-dollar car crash itself every time a squirrel or whatever runs into the road. "What would a real person do?" he says. He says that's how the car needs to react.

Levandowski heaves himself off his stool and begins pacing around the lab. He's muttering to himself.

"I thought people were the bug," is what I pick up.

Both of them want to know what I think.

What I think is that we're the guys who drive behind the car that drives itself. You want to ask a moral question, go talk to our CEO.

I pick up a dissected piece of LIDAR and twirl it between my fingers. It's a mirror attached to a long metal stem.

I say that I guess I'd choose swerve.

Clarke walks out of the room.

"What?" I call after him. "I've got a kid," I say.

Of the three of us, Clarke's the youngest. Google hired him right out of MIT. But in terms of the technology, he probably knows more than Levandowski and me combined. In college he won some kind of big government award for designing a helmet that could mind-read mice. You put the little helmet on the mouse and then put the mouse in a maze. The helmet would tell you a fraction of a second before the mouse turned a corner if it was going to turn left or right.

Levandowski settles down next to me.

We begin picking through the guts of the LIDAR. There are wires and sensors and motors and motor parts. He asks me about lunch.

"A three-hour lunch," he says.

Levandowski knows all about Julia and his stance is that he disapproves. This is because Tracy and I once invited him over for dinner and now he thinks that Tracy's great.

The whole time they joked about me like I wasn't there.

Tracy passed him the green bean salad. "You should see him with the diapers," she said. She pinched her nose and held the other hand about three feet in front of her face.

"At the office," said Levandowski, "you ask him a question and he practically dives underneath his desk."

On average, Americans spend one hundred hours a year commuting back and forth to work. Stretch that out over a lifetime and that becomes eight thousand hours. Which is one full year of life.

Start adding in all of the other car trips you take and the number skyrockets. The conservative estimate is that by the time you die, you'll have spent eight years behind the wheel.

The only things you'll have spent more time doing are working, sleeping, and watching TV.

"If you hate your commute so much," says Tracy, "get another job."

She's put the baby to sleep and we're finally getting around to dinner. The microwave beeps and she puts chicken on the table.

"But who will provide us with our bounty?" I say. I gesture at the gray chicken that looks an awful lot like last night's chicken.

"You're resourceful," she says.

This is pretty much how it goes every night. I complain about something and Tracy deflects it back at me.

"You wouldn't let us starve," she says.

I'd complain about the chicken, but I already know how that one goes. Tracy will ask me what did I expect, exactly. She'll say that it's hard work raising a kid. Then she'll remind me that it wasn't a decision that she made on her own.

She'll talk about the long and frequent conversations we had, before we even started trying to make a baby, about pulling the goalie from the net.

I liked the idea. The metaphor I guess you'd call it. By pulling the goalie we were *choosing* to let fate decide.

"Who talks like that?" Tracy said when I told her this. "We're deciding," she said.

Later that night, as we undress for bed, Tracy asks me about the phone call from earlier. She wants to know why I called and hung up.

"Phone call?" I say. The baby's sleeping in her crib at the foot of the bed. We're whispering so that we don't wake her.

"You called," says Tracy. She shows me the Caller ID.

"Huh," I say. I tell her that the phone must have dialed itself.

She wants to know, on a scale of one to ten, how would I rate that answer. "One being regular bullshit," she says, "and ten being complete bullshit."

I tell her that I'd rate it zero.

"Zero's not an option," she says.

"Then how would you rate it?" I say.

She turns off the light.

So far, Google Cars have logged more than two hundred thousand miles and still they keep crashing.

For a while their biggest problem was stop signs. The cars couldn't figure out that people were essentially aggressive drivers and that they rolled through intersections instead of stopping completely. In four-way situations the accident rate was something like seven in ten.

I was the one who came up with the workaround.

By making the AI a little more aggressive we could ensure that Google Cars would roll through stop signs before other cars. Human drivers would be forced to yield to *them*.

Focus groups basically hate them, and why shouldn't they? They're more like something from *The Terminator* than *The Jetsons*.

But accidents are down by more than 50 percent.

Next morning I'm standing over the griddle making pancakes when Tracy comes into the kitchen. Pancakes are Tracy's favorite and are something

I have a true talent for. Whenever I make pancakes they always come out perfectly round and perfectly thick.

Tracy puts the baby in the high chair and asks me "What's the occasion?"

"Can't a guy make pancakes?" I say.

"I'm not complaining," she says.

She stands next to me and tugs on the collar of her bathrobe. She's not wearing anything underneath.

We watch the butter deliquesce and the batter congeal. The smell of pancakes rises into the air. I put a short stack on Tracy's plate and tell her that sometimes phones really do dial themselves.

"There's an article on Google News," I say.

"Are we still arguing about that?" says Tracy.

"Then what are we arguing about?" I say.

Tracy shushes me. She kisses me on the cheek and then on my lips. And before I know it my hands are sliding inside her bathrobe. "You know," she says, my ear in her mouth, "you're not a bad guy when you give it half a shot."

"Neither are you," I say. My hands are moving south and my palms are becoming sweaty. There's heaviness of breath. Pancake batter spitting.

"Well," I say. "Not a guy," I say.

I tell her that she knows what I mean.

She does, she says.

"I'm an adult woman and you're an adult man," she says. "With adult responsibilities," she says.

Then she lifts the baby from the high chair, wipes food off her face, and puts her in the crib for a post-breakfast nap.

She asks if I'm going to join her in the bedroom. But by then my pancakes are burning. I'm already late for work.

We're standing in the parking lot outside of Google HQ. It's overcast and there's a flock of seagulls in the trashcans. You have to shout to be heard.

Clarke's holding a baseball and is waiting for the Prius to come around again. We've rigged this one with a modified LIDAR. When it's close enough, Clarke tosses the ball. It bounces off the Prius's hood and the Prius keeps going.

Then Levandowski tosses a soccer ball. Tires screech as the Prius jerks out of the way.

We do the test several more times. Each time the Prius hits the baseball but swerves for the soccer ball. When we present the results to Page that afternoon we tell him that the Google Car can now calculate between catastrophic and non-catastrophic collisions. In the latter case, we say, the car can now decide that the less damaging decision is to collide.

AR Detection is how Clarke pitches the new feature.

AR meaning Acceptable Risk.

Page squeezes his stapler a few more times. It's only when he puts it back on his desk that I realize that I've been holding my breath.

He tells us that he wants us to start doing road tests.

"This weekend," he says.

Out in the hall I notice that the dent in the wall has been patched but not repainted. The plaster's a different shade of white.

Levandowski's upset about something. You can tell because he keeps making these "hrm" sounds and playing with the knot in his tie.

Clarke asks him what's wrong.

"Acceptable Risk?" says Levandowski.

Clarke asks him what he'd call it.

Levandowski says, "Hrm."

Then he says that baseballs and soccer balls are one thing but that he wants to know what happens to the kid who's chasing the ball.

"Is that an Acceptable Risk?" he says.

Clarke says that nothing happens. He says that that's the whole point.

By then we've walked across the campus and are at the garage and there's the question of who's going to sign the car out for the weekend. Clarke says that he will. But Levandowski says that he doesn't trust him with it.

"Not with Mr. Acceptable Risk," he says.

While they argue, I sign the waiver and pocket the keys.

Driving the Prius home, I detour through the suburbs. It's evening and in each neighborhood there are kids chasing kids, kids chasing soccer balls, dogs, kids on bikes. It's a lot of information to process.

I wonder, what if Levandowski's right?

For humans there's a tenth of a second lag between receiving and processing information. Computers are three hundred *thousand* times faster.

That means that by the time I've seen a kid running into the street, have sent the electrical signal to my foot telling it to the hit brake, and have received the signal back from my foot saying that the brake has been pressed, a computer would have done all of it three hundred thousand times.

And yet, even for computers, there are gaps in the information.

Blind spots.

Thousandths of a second when the information is still traveling, when it's neither been processed nor received.

As I continue driving I find that I've detoured my way into San Francisco. The Golden Gate Bridge, once hulking in the distance, is now the dominant part of my skyline. Its two towers, like pyramids on either side of the bay, are shining brightly, orangely, in the sun's remaining light.

Soon I find myself outside Julia's apartment. I idle on the curb and watch the sun set. The streetlights blink on.

I kill the engine.

I press the intercom and ask Julia to let me inside.

At Google, in the lab, we literally have a checklist of things we want to make sure the technology can handle before it's ready for the public.

The list goes:

Left turns: check

Stop signs: check

The list is pretty mundane but at its bottom is the meta-category *city driving.* Because not only are city streets the most difficult type to navigate, but also because people in the city are the most unpredictable.

The litmus test of our litmus test is San Francisco.

I mean, look at a street map.

It's like someone traced over a Pollack painting.

When Julia opens the door, she's wearing a dress. It's a short, shiny, tube-like thing that's designed to show off, among other things, her breasts.

I ask what the occasion is.

She says she's going to dinner.

I ask if she wants a ride. Then we're in the backseat of the Prius. There's the glow of the LIDAR's GUI and we're watching the screen's little hourglass, waiting for the AI to boot up.

I ask Julia where we're going. My fingers are poised over the touch screen, ready to punch in the address.

"I'm going on a date," she says.

Which, of course, is obvious. Besides the dress, she's wearing a honey-and-something perfume that I've never smelled before.

I'm not surprised, but still I feel something.

Gutted, I guess.

She asks me what I ever expected. "I mean," she says, "have you even thought about this? Our situation," she says and gestures between the two of us as if what we have between us is a *situation*.

"About how unfair this is to me?" she says.

Out the window the Golden Gate's towers are lit up. There's black water in between them. Cars driving across the expanse.

"I'm not breaking up," says Julia. "If you could even call it that. We can still keep doing what we're doing."

I make a noise of assent.

She names a restaurant on Embarcadero. The car starts driving. We go past other parked cars, under streetlights, up a hill.

After I drop Julia off, I let the car drive me home. I sit in the backseat and watch the moonlight on the water. Even in the dark you can see the waves breaking toward the shore.

There are other cars on the road though not that many. As we pass each other, my car and the other cars, I wonder what this looks like to them, the other drivers in the other cars. This driverless Prius, with its steering wheel jerking itself, and its man in the backseat gazing out the window, his forehead pressed against the glass? What will it look like in ten years when all the cars are like this?

All those autonomous cars with their LIDAR masts, AR augmentation, collision detection units, lasers, radars, HUDS, GUIs, infrared cameras, inertial measurements, and 6-D stereo-vision systems? Cars that never get lost and can drive themselves, down to the millimeter, exactly in the middle of the lane? What will it be like for us when we we're no longer driving ourselves?

I think about Tracy and the baby and myself riding safely in the backseat of a driverless car just like this one. I think about how tomorrow we can all be taken for a ride.

For a while I'm buoyed by the thought.

One of the first things that Julia taught me is that science is the expression of what we've learned to keep from fooling ourselves.

"Poetry," she said, "is also the expression of what we've learned to keep from fooling ourselves."

We were naked in her bed and I'd asked why she was studying what she was studying. Why poetry and machines? I asked if she ever read just for fun.

I told her that when I was a kid I used to read for fun all the time.

"When I was a kid," I said, and she put her finger on my lips, shushed me. "You're not a child," she said.

She began reading to me.

She read me that Emerson poem.

She said, "Things are in the saddle and ride mankind."

She said, "Go, blind worm, go."

And I did, eventually.

SPOOKY ACTION AT A DISTANCE

We were surprised, of course, that when we built our time machine it turned out to be a DeLorean. We took it apart, put it back together, didn't matter. Looked at the blueprints, looked at the silver car. Scratched our heads. A joke? A prank? Sabotage? If sabotage, then it had backfired. The DeLorean worked.

We drove it out of the laboratory, into the parking lot, set the chronometer, and stepped on the gas. When we arrived, we were exactly when we wanted to be. Thirty minutes earlier, our own past.

We parked the DeLorean behind a dumpster, hid in the bushes, and spied on ourselves. There we were, earlier Dr. Hu and earlier me, lab-locked and bending over our blueprints, scratching our heads. After that we did pretty much what you'd expect anyone to do with a time machine. We killed Hitler. Smothered him in his crib.

We smothered lots of history's evil people. Bin Laden, Mao, Cheney, Robespierre, Attila the Hun. Even though we had the moral imperative it wasn't easy killing babies, so we saved people too to balance it out. We saved JFK, RFK, MLK. Saved Franz Ferdinand, Marie Antoinette. You'd be surprised how many people can be saved just by pulling up in a DeLorean and shouting *Duck*.

Also surprising was that there seemed to be no negative consequences. No double-occupancy problems, no grandfather paradoxes, no quantum entanglements. Fixing history was easy, like smoothing out the wrinkles in your bed.

This is how I explained it to my wife, the underwear model. I ran my fingers across our sheets. I told her that every time Dr. Hu and I returned to our time everything was pretty much as we'd left it except for a little bit better. History wasn't something heavy that everyone had to carry around with them, a backpack full of broken parts.

For example, take you, I said. In another timeline you were you but not an underwear model. You were a kindergarten teacher. Your father died when you were twelve. In another timeline, I said, you were you but not someone you would recognize. You got pregnant in high school, drove drunk, got paralyzed below the waist. In another timeline you were never born.

What about you? she asked of me.

I listened to the cicadas singing their seventeen-year song.

I said that in another timeline Dr. Hu and I had won the Nobel Prize in physics. We went public with our time machine and now everyone had one parked in their garage. In another timeline Dr. Hu and I were villains. We did everything that we did in this timeline except exactly the opposite. Saved Hitler, killed Kennedy, ruled over all of creation from a throne of human skulls. In another timeline, I said, Dr. Hu and I were nobody. Our DeLorean turned out to be just a DeLorean. We blamed each other for our failure, stopped speaking.

In that timeline, I said, I'm married to you, the kindergarten teacher. We live in a house just like this one and are probably lying together in bed just like this. But in that timeline, I said, we are not happy. I'm a failure and you're a kindergarten teacher. We just had a fight. It doesn't matter what we fought about because the gist is that I'm a failure and you're a kindergarten teacher and you're happy enough with what we've got.

But in that timeline I'm aware that there are other timelines where I'm not a failure. I'm aware that there are timelines where I'm a time traveler, a Nobel Prize winner, an evil dictator, where you're an underwear model. In those timelines we made all of the right decisions, somehow, and didn't go off track.

And when I think about those timelines I get so mad. Because what if I had done something differently, married someone else, gotten a smarter lab partner, done better on my college admission tests, and ended up a success?

Or what if it had been a decision that I had made even earlier, something small, that had screwed everything up? Like when I was in elementary school and made fun of Margaret for being adopted. For not being white? What if I'd chosen not to join in with all of the other kids who were teasing her? Or what if I'd decided to stand up for her, told them to stop because we were neighbors, we were in homeroom together, and she had always been pretty nice? What if there was one small-hearted decision from which all of my other wrong decisions came, these decisions growing and growing the distance between what I wanted and what I got until it became so unbreachable that not even a DeLorean could cross?

SOME ZOMBIES

After Super Walmart, Charles and Kara came home and found zombies in their front yard. There were like one hundred zombies trampling their lawn. Zombies on the neighbors' lawns and on all the lawns. Most of the neighbors were zombies. Some of them moaned. "Zombies are cool," said Charles. Zombies stood in the driveway and in front of the garage. One was eating a cat. Kara honked the horn. Zombies stood. It was October, and yellow and orange-red leaves fell off the trees and onto zombies. Charles and Kara had been dating a year and a half. They were having relationship problems. Charles was five years older than Kara and had asked her to marry him. In a panic, she said yes. She was in her mid-twenties and unprepared for life's vicissitudes. She had imagined that she would be able to sleep around until she was in her thirties. At least. Somehow, she felt, someone had tricked her. "Honk the horn," said Charles.

"I honked the horn." She honked again. Zombies found a living person. It was Mr. Lau. They pulled him off his bike and tore him to pieces. The blood sprayed ten feet in the air. Another thing that she disliked about Charles was his pushiness.

"I have to pee," said Charles.

Zombies were on a killing rampage. "We can't get married," said Kara. "I can't." One of the zombies was the piano teacher, Mrs. Young. Her jaw hung from her face in a permanent gape. Off and on Kara had taken lessons for eight years but was never very good. "You have to practice your scales," Mrs. Young used to say. "Play your scales. Play C minor, play C minor now."

Now Mrs. Young threw a dismembered limb at Kara's car. The limb landed on the car, left a blood streak, and rolled to the ground.

"What about our plans?" said Charles. "Our plans for a long and happy life. A life sanctified by the blessings of God." Charles crossed his legs. When he bought his Coke, Kara told him not to super-size. He super-sized it anyway. The empty yellow wax-paper cup rolled beneath the seat.

"Pee in this," said Kara. She reached under the seat and shoved the cup at Charles. "You never listen to me," she said. "I want a secular service." She felt sleepy and wanted take a hot bath.

Zombies broke into Kara and Charles's house. They smashed down the door and carried out the television, the VCR, the stereo system. They flung clothing across the yard. A zombie ripped apart Kara's favorite bra. Another wore Charles's corduroy pants.

"My pants," said Charles. He frowned and looked at his pants. There were dirt stains near the ankles. "Listen, maybe if you honk the horn longer. Press on it for a long time." He reached across the seat and held down the horn. Kara's father didn't like Charles. He called him effeminate. Charles was a computer programmer. He programmed pop-up advertisements for the Internet. He had programmed more than one thousand. Whenever Kara was on the Internet and an advertisement popped up, Charles told her which ones were his. "I made that one," he said. "I made that one and that one and that one and that one."

"Not to Charles," Kara's father said when she told him about the marriage. He was in low-security prison for tax evasion. Kara told him during her weekly visit. "Don't marry him just because you're upset with me," he said.

"I hate you," said Kara. Charles turned away from her and a zombie pressed its rotten genitals against the car window.

"Okay," said Charles. "Fine." Another zombie leaned against the car and exposed itself, and then came another and another. Rampaging zombies crowded around the car. They pushed their bodies against it and climbed on top of it until it was completely covered: a green-red, pukish, rotting, fleshy lump. "Hate me," said Charles. "Fine. Fine. Fine."

A few weeks later Charles and Kara went back to Super Walmart. They bought bed skirts, decorative pillows, down comforters and duvets, electric blankets, throw rugs, slip covers, panel curtains, floor lamps, wall lamps, touch lamps, ceiling fans, sectional sofas, microfiber ottomans and faux-leather chaise lounge chairs, bar stools, wine chillers, rice cookers, slow cookers, jug blenders, citrus juicers, electric can openers, sonic toothbrushes, oral irrigators, extra-wide hair straighteners, self-cleaning shavers, deep cleaners, wet/dry upright vacuums, yard rakes, garden claws, oscillating sprinklers, bamboo fencing, spade shovels, pick mattocks, corded and cordless screwdrivers, lithium-ion inflators, handheld GPS navigators, cellular telephones, digital music recorders, DVD players, sling boxes, flat-panel televisions, home entertainment systems. They bought ninety-day replacement plans. Three-year warranties, lifetime warranties, etc.

VICISSITUDES, CA

1

Brandon and Kara went hiking but were unprepared for the physical challenge. "Hiking is hard work," said Kara. She cupped her hands and drank from a limpid mountain stream.

"But it's awesome," she said.

"Nature rocks," said Brandon.

They were in the San Gabriel Mountains and from their elevation could see Los Angeles and the smog in the distance.

Nature, he thought, is good because it's simple and expansive.

Brandon came to the mountains to find enlightenment. Enlightenment, he learned from his yoga teacher, could be found in nature.

Kara thought Brandon needed stimulation. She liked him, she said, but was tired of his moodiness and constant napping.

Kara took off her overshirt and sat on a rock in the sun. Underneath, she wore a tank top that Brandon admired on account of her breasts.

Kara has nice breasts, he thought, even if we are just friends.

A cloud moved away from the sun and a yellow sunbeam shined on a nearby tree.

"Look at that tree," said Kara.

She pointed to the tall, luminous pine.

"There's so much meaning in that tree."

2

The next day Kara was sick with dysentery.

Brandon visited her at the hospital.

He gave her a bouquet of flowers and asked how it was going.

"I have dysentery," said Kara, "because microorganisms have invaded my intestines via my stomach."

"Montezuma's Revenge," said Charles.

"The lesson," said Charles, "is never to drink from a limpid mountain stream."

Great, thought Brandon, Charles is here.

3

A few weeks later Brandon met Kara and Charles for dinner at a macrobiotic restaurant on La Brea.

They sat at a small round table and looked at their menus.

"I love macrobiotic food," said Kara.

Charles said, "Macrobiotic food is my favorite."

Brandon didn't know about macrobiotic food.

He looked at his menu.

What's seitan? he thought.

"I'm thinking of ordering the tempeh with miso-cured tofu cheese," said Kara.

"On ciabatta?" said Charles. "Ciabatta is a gluten," Charles said.

Charles was a personal trainer.

Not so long ago he moved to Los Angeles from Orange County to expand his client base. This is how he met Kara.

First she was his client.

Then his girlfriend.

Soon they'd be moving in together.

"But I've lost five pounds," said Kara.

"Because of the dysentery," she said.

"In fluids," said Charles.

Charles said, "Fluids don't count."

Kara pulled her hair away from her neck. Her neck was slender and featured an array of beauty marks.

"Then I'll get the seitan wrap," she said.

Charles ordered the chopped salad.

When it was Brandon's turn he couldn't decide.

In a panic he ordered the tuna roll.

But I hate sushi, he thought when the meals came out.

Charles said something about politics.

"I dislike the president," he said.

"Garfield was my favorite president," said Brandon.

"James A. Garfield?" said Kara. "President from March to September of 1881?"

"From Ohio?" she said.

"That's the one," said Brandon. He said, "I think he would have proven to be an effective leader if he'd been given the chance."

Charles put his hand on Kara's knee.

"That's funny," said Charles. "Garfield's killer, Charles Guiteau, is my favorite presidential assassin, and it's not just because we share a name."

He said, "Did you know that Guiteau killed the president because he was sexually frustrated?"

"How awful," said Kara.

Brandon poked his tuna roll.

"Don't you agree, Brandon?" said Charles.

"Agree?"

"That sexual frustration is awful."

"I thought Guiteau killed Garfield because he wanted to be ambassador to France," said Brandon.

"Please," said Charles.

He said, "Everyone wants to be ambassador to France."

4

The next day Brandon woke up to the bright morning sun shining through his bedroom window.

He walked to his couch and napped until lunch.

After lunch Brandon looked for jobs on the Internet.

He read, Financial Analyst, Portfolio Associate, Dental Receptionist, Detention Services Officer, Helicopter Repair.

Just like the day before, and the day before that, and the day before that, and the day before that, there were no listings for Ethnomusicologist.

Ethnomusicology is all I am passionate about, thought Brandon.

Brandon had recently finished his PhD in Ethnomusicology. Often he wondered why it seemed like no one besides himself realized how important it was to study music in conjunction with certain ethnographic and social phenomena.

He thought about all his Ethnomusicologist heroes.

Why would the world not want more Ethnomusicologists?

Soon he found himself looking at pornography.

To cheer himself up he went to the movies.

There were explosions.

Romance.

When he walked out of the theater he felt even more depressed.

Film could have been a viable artistic medium, he thought, but had shed all its loftier aspirations for pure financial gain.

I was entertained, he thought, but I wasn't moved.

5

Brandon went to Kara and Charles's housewarming.

Local business entrepreneurs and minor celebrities loitered in the living room and on the patio.

Since when, thought Brandon, did Kara befriend so many minor celebrities?

"Charles just opened his own athletic club," said Kara.

"We're considering a franchise," she said.

They had just moved into a new apartment in Silver Lake.

To celebrate they bought a Pekingese and named it Chu Chu.

Miranda July lived a floor above.

The apartment was decorated with modern furniture. Brandon wandered over to a sleek-looking bookshelf and looked at the bright and varicolored books.

Above the bookshelf was a painting.

Yellow, orange, a slash of red.

"Rothko," said Kara.

"It's just a print," she said.

Miranda July stood alone at the drinks table.

She looked disinterestedly into her cup.

"That's Miranda July," said Kara.

"I liked her movies," said Brandon, "and her books."

"Thank you," said Miranda July.

"They all occurred to me naturally," she said, "as when a plant springs from the soil or when an animal gives birth to a litter of baby animals."

Charles walked through the living room with a platter of cocktail shrimp.

Chu Chu trailed behind.

"Oh no!" said Kara. She said that Charles wasn't supposed to serve the shrimp until after the crudités.

She chased Charles and Chu Chu back into the kitchen.

Miranda July asked Brandon what he did for a living.

"Ethnomusicologist," he said.

"Unemployed," he said.

"Of course," said Miranda July.

She told Brandon that all worthwhile professions were practically unemployable. Then she told him about an uncle who was an analytic philosopher. He lived in squalor until he died.

"Pneumonia," she said.

"It was probably very treatable," she said.

A hired pianist began playing Bach's *Well-Tempered Clavier*.

Brandon told Miranda July that the piece had been a favorite of his favorite Ethnomusicologist, the great Carl Stumpf.

Miranda July nodded.

"Music is the world-language of feeling," she said.

6

Later that week the phone rang.

It was Miranda July.

"Of course," said Brandon.

"I love lunch," he said.

He stood in front of his closet and looked at his clothing. He thought about calling Kara then remembered that she and Charles had gone to Puerto Vallarta for the long weekend.

What does one wear? he thought.

Eventually he chose a dark shirt and thought about Miranda July.

Sexually.

7

"Hello, Miranda July," said Brandon.

"Hello, Brandon," said Miranda July.

Miranda July had chosen an outdoor table at the café and looked especially pale and elegant beneath the bright and cloudless sky.

Brandon said something about the weather.

"Seventy degrees and sunny," said Miranda July.

"It was overcast this morning," said Brandon.

"The marine layer," said Miranda July.

Miranda July wore a black scarf which she took off and folded in her lap.

Brandon twisted his napkin.

Miranda July checked her phone.

She sent a text message.

A white van pulled to the curb and several paparazzi jumped out.

"Look!" said one. "Miranda July is eating lunch!"

They began assaulting Miranda July with bewildering flashes.

"With whom is Miranda July eating lunch?" said another.

The cameras flashed on Brandon.

"Look at the shabbiness of his clothing," said a paparazzo. "The collar of his shirt is fraying. His jeans are ill-fitting. His shoes are nearly worn to the sole."

"He must be a blossoming actor," said another.

"A struggling artist."

"An independent musician."

When their lunch came out, Miranda July squeezed ketchup onto her French fries. "These French fries are horrible," she said.

"Taste them," she said. "They're limp and tasteless."

Brandon thought the fries tasted okay but told Miranda July that she should send them back if she disliked them.

"One must not settle," he said.

"I disagree," said Miranda July.

She squirted more ketchup on the fries and continued eating.

She said, "An inability to settle can be the source of great unhappiness."

8

"Puerto Vallarta is amazing," said Kara.

As she walked, her hair clacked in tight, beaded braids.

"There are breathtaking sunsets and jungle-covered mountains," she said.

Kara and Brandon were walking Chu Chu to the dog park near her new apartment.

Her new engagement ring burst in the sun.

Brandon told her that he'd had lunch with Miranda July.

"How'd it go?" asked Kara.

"She paid," he said.

Kara scooped Chu Chu's poop into a plastic bag.

Back at his apartment, Brandon watched a news report about gray whales. The gray whales were dead and kept washing up on a nearby beach. Their smell menaced the surrounding beach communities.

The TV showed pictures of volunteers rolling the whales back to sea.

The news reporter explained that each time the volunteers rolled the whales out to sea they were washed up again somewhere else along the coast.

She interviewed a volunteer.

"This time," said the volunteer, "we're going to roll the whales out to sea and attach them to boats via meat hooks. The boats will drag the whales even further out into the ocean. With luck, they'll be eaten by sharks and other sea animals."

They stood on a beach where the whale corpses moldered in the background.

The reporter blinked into the camera. Her nose and mouth were hidden behind a carbon mask but her eyes were brown.

Kara has brown eyes, Brandon observed.

He remembered the last time he and Kara had gone to the beach.

Brandon had rubbed suntan lotion onto Kara's shoulders.

Kara had rubbed suntan lotion onto his.

But now, he thought. Now Charles will be the only one to rub suntan lotion onto Kara's shoulders.

9

Brandon, Kara, Charles, and Miranda July all went to the horse racing track in Hollywood.

They sat in the box seats.

Chu Chu sat in Kara's lap.

"Horse racing is the sport of kings," said Charles. He flagged down a waiter and ordered more ice for their juleps.

"But it's dangerous," he said.

"Per one hundred thousand participants," said Kara, "it has the highest number of deaths."

"A blood sport," said Charles.

Miranda July sat next to Brandon. Her hands were folded in her lap.

There are Miranda July's hands, thought Brandon. I would offer to hold them but I don't know her intentions.

He pondered the artist's inscrutable self.

Charles talked about his athletic club.

"I've just hired an assistant," he said. "His name is Javier and he has long golden hair and the most perfect biceps I've ever seen."

The gates opened and the horses charged out.

"Which one did you bet on?" asked Kara.

"Blaze of Enchantment," said Miranda July. "He's currently running neck-and-neck with Apache Sunrise."

"Apache Sunrise is a shoo-in," said Charles.

He said, "He was sired by Sierra's Sweet Rain."

The horses rounded the far corner and thundered toward the grandstand.

As they came nearer, Chu Chu leaped from Kara's lap.

He bounded onto the track and was trampled by the thoroughbreds.

"Chu Chu!" said Kara.

"Blaze of Enchantment!"

"Apache Sunrise!"

The lead horses collapsed in a pile on top of the Pekingese.

Enraged, the other spectators began pelting Brandon, Kara, Charles, and Miranda July with their losing betting slips.

On the racetrack, a team of stablehands began untangling the scrum of jockeys and horses.

"Chu Chu," said Kara.

Charles wrapped her in his commiserative embrace.

10

"Poor Chu Chu," said Charles. "My only consolation is that Blaze of Enchantment and Apache Sunrise will never race again."

"Nor will Moonshadow," said Miranda July.

"Nor Lady Boots," said Brandon.

"Nor Peach Blossom," said Charles.

"Nor Afternoon Delight," said Miranda July.

After the ceremony Kara stood alone by the punch-and-crackers table and stroked her jar of ashes.

11

The principal looked at Brandon's resume.

"It says here," said the principal, "that you're an Ethnomusicologist."

"I am," said Brandon.

"Do you care to explain?"

"Ethnomusicology?"

"Yes," said the principal.

Brandon explained.

"And you propose to teach Ethnomusicology to elementary school children?"

On the wall behind the principal were portraits of the school's previous principals. They gazed sternly at Brandon.

"Yes," said Brandon.

"Maybe," he said.

The principal wrote something in his notebook.

"And what about the recorder?" said the principal.

He said, "Can you teach the recorder?"

"I can play the recorder," said Brandon, "or the sweet flute as it was called in the eighteenth century."

The principal reached into his desk and pulled out a recorder.

Brandon took the beige Bakelite instrument and blew into the fipple.

Out came a cascade of sweetly sour notes.

12

"Miranda July?" said Brandon.

"Yes, Brandon," said Miranda July.

"Is it true what they say about us in the tabloids?"

"No."

"Are you sure?"

"Of course I am."

"Not even a little bit true?"

"How could something be a little bit true?"

"Well—" said Brandon.

"Well what?"

He said, "We do spend a lot of time together."

After Miranda July left his apartment, Brandon continued lying on his couch and continued thinking about it.

But we really do spend a lot of time together, is what he thought.

13

Brandon phoned his mother in Cleveland.

"I don't feel special," he said.

His mother told him that he was special.

But she was his mother.

Another week passed and he heard nothing from the job search, nor did he hear anything from Miranda July.

14

Kara told Brandon that she didn't know what to tell him about Miranda July. "But when it comes to the job search," she said, "maybe you should expand your horizons."

They were at Charles's athletic club.

Kara wore a black unitard and was on the step machine.

Her face was red from stepping.

"Ethnomusicology is diverse," said Brandon.

"It's multidisciplinary," he said.

On the other side of the gym Miranda July was doing dumbbell squats in front of the long mirror. Brandon thought she was watching him.

"But maybe you should apply for other types of jobs?" said Kara.

"Charles could help you," she said.

Brandon told her that he refused to work for The Man.

"The Man?" said Kara.

"The establishment culture," said Brandon.

Kara told Brandon that she knew what The Man was.

"What year do you live in?" she said. She told Brandon that history had long proven the institution to be ubiquitous.

Meanwhile, Charles's new assistant, Javier, approached Miranda July.

He placed the hand of his well-muscled arm above her buttocks and demonstrated a more efficient squat.

"Bend at the hips," he said.

"The hips?" said Miranda July.

"Your fine curvaceous hips."

Well, thought Brandon.

Back at his apartment he continued searching for jobs on the Internet.

Soon he was looking at pictures of naked girls.

The naked girls touched themselves. The naked girls touched each other. Sometimes the naked girls touched each other with cubes of ice.

15

The owners of the lamed horses were suing Charles and Kara.

"It's outrageous," said Charles.

"They want eleven million," he said.

Charles chopped vegetables in his kitchen. He was making a salad to go with his steak. He chopped tomatoes and onions, zucchinis and bell peppers.

He chopped with zeal.

"But we're going to file a counterclaim," said Kara.

Her knife wavered over an avocado.

She said, "The racetrack was not properly barricaded."

"The lawyers agree," said Charles. "A post-and-rail fence is not an adequate barrier."

"Lawyers?" said Brandon.

Charles: "My team of expensive lawyers."

Brandon's father had been a lawyer. He'd practiced corporate law until he was disbarred for tax evasion. Currently he was serving time in the penitentiary in Chillicothe, OH, which had once been the prison to Charles Manson.

Brandon liked to point out that Charles Manson was a very important figure in North American Ethnomusicology.

"Charles Manson had close ties to the Beach Boys," said Brandon.

He said, "He contributed lyrics to the song 'Never Learn Not To Love.'"

"Everyone knows that," said Charles. "His contribution was uncredited. The song was originally entitled 'Cease To Exist.'"

Kara changed the subject.

"Let's change the subject," she said.

She asked if anyone had heard about the gray whales.

"Back again," said Brandon.

"Those poor people," said Kara. "But I suppose everyone must suffer. After all suffering is the counterpoint to happiness."

Everyone agreed and Kara served dinner.

After dinner she announced that she was joining the job search.

"Lawyers are expensive," she said.

"As are weddings," said Charles. "Lawyers and weddings."

Kara proposed a toast.

16

Brandon went to the grocery store.

He pushed his cart down the frozen food aisle and selected frozen pizza, frozen pot pie, frozen lasagna, frozen buffalo wings, frozen mixed vegetables, frozen Hot Pockets.

Then he steered his cart into the condiments aisle and reached for a bottle of ketchup.

On the other end of the aisle Miranda July was reaching for a bottle of mustard.

"Miranda July," said Brandon.

"Brandon," said Miranda July.

They pushed their carts toward each other and met in the center of the aisle in front of the salsa and mayonnaise.

Miranda July's cart was filled with cans of tuna fish.

She wore a white T-shirt and her breasts were two small cones that pointed at Brandon's chest.

He tried to imagine them naked.

Miranda July's breasts, he thought.

Veil of cotton, he thought.

"Brandon?" said Miranda July.

"Um," said Brandon.

"It's good to see you," he said.

He asked Miranda July about the tuna fish.

She explained that it was for a performance piece.

She said, "I'm going to cover myself in tuna fish and molder on an expensive beach."

"Like the whales," she said.

"What beach?" asked Brandon.

"Point Dume."

"Why?"

Miranda July: "Art doesn't ask why."

17

Brandon paid for his groceries and went back to his apartment. His landlord was waiting for him on the front steps.

"Your rent is due," said the landlord.

She sat with her walking cane across her knees and a cigarette burning between two fingers.

"It was due last week," she said.

Brandon shifted his groceries from one arm to the other.

He shifted them back.

"I don't have enough money," he said.

The landlord grinned.

Her teeth glinted under the blank, gray sky.

"How much did those cost you?"

"My groceries?" said Brandon.

"Your groceries," she said.

"I don't know," he said.

"I guess about one hundred dollars," he said.

The smoke rose off her cigarette.

"I want them," said the landlord.

"My groceries?"

"Yes," she said.

"Give me your groceries," she said.

18

"Be an empty rice bowl," said the yoga instructor.

Brandon bent himself into the position.

He pressed his hands and feet to the mat and pushed upward.

What he liked most about yoga was the mat. When he stood on it he felt as if he were on his own private rubber island.

I am an empty bowl of rice, he thought.

His hips and buttocks strained toward the ceiling.

Next to him Kara did the same.

The yoga instructor strolled by and stopped to comment on Kara's form.

"Good," said the yoga instructor.

"Feel the fireflies in your stomach," he said.

The yoga instructor's bare foot was planted on Brandon's mat. His big toe was leveled directly below Brandon's nose.

Empty bowl of rice, thought Brandon.

Empty bowl of rice, he thought.

Private island, he thought.

"Brandon?" said the yoga instructor. "What's wrong?"

After the class, Brandon arranged his face into a smile.

He pulled his lips toward his cheeks, his cheeks toward his forehead, and his forehead toward his occipital bone.

"What are you doing?" said Kara.

"Smiling," he said.

"It looks painful."

Kara tied her shoes and continued telling Brandon about her new job. "Which is why yoga is good," she said, "because work puts so much strain on the body. After work, my neck is strained. My upper back is strained. My lower back is strained."

"But you must be happy to have found a job so quickly."

"Not happy," said Kara.

She crossed her legs and began tying the other shoe.

"What I feel is more like relief," she said.

She said, "Charles and I are relieved to have the extra money. Our legal costs are mounting and so are our wedding costs. The wedding decorator wants to know what we want for centerpieces. Charles wants floating tea candles. I want fresh flowers. Obviously we can't have both."

"Obviously," said Brandon.

But the distinction bothered him long after he returned home.

Why couldn't one have both floating tea candles and fresh flowers?

He stood in front of his empty refrigerator and gazed into its darkest depths.

What a cruel world this is, he thought, where one must constantly be forced to choose between two equally attractive but competing desires. I can continue being an Ethnomusicologist, he thought. Or I can eat.

19

Vast greenness.

Brandon stood at the tee box and gazed out onto the fairway.

The hole was a long dogleg.

Sand traps pooled in the distance.

"What do you think?" said Charles. He pondered his shot and consulted with Javier. "Which club should I use?"

Javier crossed his muscular arms, cupped his chin, and brooded.

"Three-wood," he said.

"My thought exactly," said Charles.

He said, "The three-wood has a long flexible shaft, a nicely shaped head, and a thick, sturdy hosel."

Charles swung the club and the ball disappeared.

It was Brandon's turn.

He swung his club at the ball and missed.

He swung and missed again.

"Two strokes," said Charles.

"The trick," said Charles, "is to keep your head down and follow through with your swing."

Brandon swung again and this time the club connected.

The ball bounced a few yards before settling in the grass.

"Good," said Charles.

"Well not good," he said, "but you know what I mean."

Charles and Javier mounted the cart and drove ahead to look for their shots.

Meanwhile, Brandon continued hitting his ball up the dogleg. When he finally came around to the other side of the trees he saw the cart parked in a secluded grove behind the green.

Charles and Javier were in the cart and from a distance they seemed to be embracing.

Charles seemed to be embracing Javier.

Javier seemed to be embracing Charles.

And it seemed as if they were doing something with their mouths, as if their mouths were also embracing.

Shocking, thought Brandon.

He thought, I am absolutely shocked.

But when he thought about it later he was somehow not surprised. I was shocked, he thought, but I'm not surprised.

20

Brandon met Kara for lunch the next day.

They sat on a bench in front of Kara's office building and watched the reflections of clouds drift across the big mirrored windows.

"How'd it go?" said Kara.

She'd packed sandwiches for both of them, peanut butter and jelly for herself and just peanut butter for Brandon because he didn't like jelly.

"Fine," said Brandon.

"Charles is going to help you with the job search?"

Brandon nodded.

"Excellent," said Kara.

"Charles is so generous," she said.

She bit into her sandwich and a large gob of jelly flew out. Brandon picked up his napkin and pressed it to her blouse.

"Kara," he said.

He said, "There's something I need to tell you about Charles."

As the purple stain spread across her breast Brandon told her everything he'd seen out on the golf course.

21

"Do you solemnly swear to tell the truth, the whole truth, and nothing but the truth, so help you God?"

After Miranda July testified about Chu Chu and the racehorses it was Brandon's turn.

He sat on the hard wooden bench and felt the judge's eyes upon him.

He felt the jury's eyes, the lawyers' eyes, the bailiff's eyes, the court reporter's eyes, the horse owners' eyes, Miranda July's eyes, Javier's eyes, Charles's eyes, and Kara's eyes.

He felt Kara's eyes most of all.

Kara held Charles's hand and glared at Brandon.

The interrogation began.

22

Brandon described the scene the best he could.

There was the noise, the stink, the heat, and the thick cloud of dust settling over the grandstand after Chu Chu had been trampled.

There were horses splayed on the beaten dirt track.

There were jockeys piled on top of them.

And from underneath it all, there was the handle end of Chu Chu's leash.

The lawyer for the horse owners paced in front of the jury box.

Twelve representative heads swung back and forth.

"And your father?" she said.

"Would you please tell us about your father?" she said.

"My father?" said Brandon. "He wasn't at the racetrack."

"Why not?" said the lawyer.

"Because he lives in Ohio."

"You mean in prison," said the lawyer.

She said, "He lives in prison in Ohio."

She stopped pacing and cracked open the red slash of lipstick on her face, revealing two rows of very white teeth.

"Let the record show," she said, "that Brandon's father is a criminal."

She said, "Let the record further show that his mother's been calling him but that he hasn't returned her calls."

Charles's lawyer tried to object but his objection was overruled.

"Your soul is narrow," the horse owners' lawyer told Brandon.

She said, "Your character is flawed."

Across the courtroom Kara continued to glare.

23

Brandon pulled his couch onto the sidewalk.

He wrote *$100* on a piece of cardboard and leaned it against the couch's cushions.

Then he went back into his apartment and brought out his mattress, his bed frame, his table, his chairs, his television stand, and his bookshelf.

He priced everything to sell and sat on the steps waiting for buyers to come.

Soon two teenage boys appeared.

Each was pushing a bike that appeared to be stolen. The bikes were girls' bikes, pink with flower decals and silver streamers streaming from the handlebars.

The teenagers dropped the bikes in the grass and flopped down on Brandon's couch.

"How much?" said one.

Brandon told him.

"How about fifty?" said the other.

"Fine," said Brandon.

Then the teenagers assaulted Brandon.

One punched him in the stomach and brought him to the ground. The other kicked him in the face.

While Brandon writhed on the ground the teenagers picked up his couch and walked away with it.

They left their bikes in the grass.

Soon Brandon picked himself up off the sidewalk.

He picked up the bikes and priced them *$10* each.

24

"Your couch?" said Miranda July.

"Yes," said Brandon.

"The teenagers," he said.

They were sitting on the floor of Brandon's apartment. Brandon pressed a beer bottle to his swollen nose.

On the TV on the floor across from them a news reporter was standing in front of the courthouse.

A picture of Chu Chu flashed on the screen.

"How's your nose?" said Miranda July.

"I think it's broken," said Brandon.

Miranda July stared at his bruise. Her irises were two black disks that scanned back and forth across Brandon's face.

She asked Brandon if she could touch it.

She said, "I've never touched a broken nose."

She cupped her hands over his nose.

"It's warm," said Miranda July.

"Warmer than a normal nose," she said, "and firmer than I expected for something that's broken."

A tear ran down Brandon's cheek.

25

Charles and Kara stepped out of the courthouse and were greeted by reporters. The reporters pushed toward them and asked them how they felt about the verdict.

"Victorious," said Charles.

He said, "This is a victory for dog owners everywhere. It proves that post-and-rail fences are not adequate barriers for horse racing tracks. We hope that horse racing track owners everywhere see the message that has been sent today and replace their post-and-rail fences with more substantial fencing."

Kara reached into her purse and removed a framed picture of Chu Chu.

"Imagine," she said, "if it had not been our little dog that had wandered onto the racetrack but that it had been somebody's child who had been crushed to death under the hooves of so many horses."

Kara gazed intently into the cameras and continued fondling the picture of Chu Chu.

26

"Kara looks fat," said Miranda July.

"It's the TV," said Brandon.

"I agree," said Miranda July.

She said, "TV makes everyone fat."

27

That night Brandon had a nightmare.

It began, as so many dreams do, as a dream of naked girls.

The naked girls were washing cars. Some washed the cars with hoses. Others washed the cars with sponges.

Eventually a school bus appeared for the naked girls to wash.

They lathered and sprayed the school bus and when it emerged from the cloud of soap one of the naked girls told Brandon to get in.

"In the bus?" said Brandon.

"Get in," she said.

Brandon got in the bus and said hello to Miranda July who was driving it.

"Where are we going?"

"Home," said Miranda July.

But as the bus began traveling it became clear that Miranda July wasn't taking Brandon back to Ohio.

There was rainforest outside the bus's windows.

"Where are we?" said Brandon.

"Puerto Vallarta," said Miranda July.

"It's beautiful," said Brandon.

"Indeed," said Miranda July.

"But it's also dangerous," she said.

As soon as she said this, three people stepped out onto the road in front of the bus. Each wore a red balaclava and carried an AK-47.

"See," said Miranda July.

She brought the bus to a stop.

The guerillas boarded the bus and pointed their guns at Brandon's face.

"Give us your nose," said one.

This one was well-muscled and had a familiar voice.

"Charles?" said Brandon.

Charles took off his balaclava.

"Give us your nose," he said.

Kara took off her balaclava.

"Your lying nose," she said.

Then the third person stepped forward and swiped the nose off Brandon's face.

"Brandon," said his landlord.

"I've got your nose," she said.

28

When Brandon woke up his nose was throbbing.

He found a note taped to his door.

The teenagers wanted their bikes back. If the bicycles weren't returned, the teenagers said, they were going to mess Brandon up.

They made a short list of the things that they'd do to him.

We'll slice off your ears.

We'll feed your ears to the birds.

We'll invert your knees.

Below the list was a picture of an earless stickman with inverted knees.

Stickbirds on the ground were eating the stickman's ears.

Though the drawing was crude, the teenagers had been able to render the stickman's obvious pain.

Brandon decided not to be home when the teenagers came back.

He rolled up his yoga mat and went to the yoga studio. But when he arrived there, the woman at the counter told him that he couldn't take the class.

"Your nose," she said.

"It's bleeding," she said.

Brandon touched his nose and saw that it was indeed bleeding. He also realized that he couldn't feel it. His nose was numb.

"May I have a tissue?" he said.

The woman gave him the box.

Brandon sat on the bench outside the yoga studio and rolled tissues into his nose. He thought about going home.

But then he thought about the frowning stickman.

29

Later Kara came out of the yoga studio and found Brandon sitting on the bench. Her skin shone with a lucent halo of sweat.

"Brandon?" she said.

She asked what he was doing there.

Then she asked what had happened to his face.

"Teenagers," said Brandon.

"How horrible," said Kara.

"But," she said, "I suppose you deserve it. After all it's like they say: An eye for an eye, a tooth for a tooth, a hand for a hand, a foot for a foot, etc."

"They?" said Brandon.

"Yes," said Kara.

She said, "That's what *they* say."

"And Charles?" said Brandon.

"Charles and they," said Kara.

Then she told Brandon that the teenagers must have been the agents of karmic justice, doling out punishment for the lies that Brandon had been spreading about Charles.

She also told Brandon that he was mostly forgiven.

"After all," she said, "forgiveness is the better part of valor."

"Not discretion?" said Brandon.

He took out a tissue to see if his nose was still bleeding.

It was.

"Forgiveness," said Kara.

She told Brandon that she forgave him because his jealousy of Charles was understandable. Charles was successful. He was a small business owner. Brandon, on the other hand, was something else entirely. He was like an artist, she said, but without skills or ambition.

To show how forgiven he was, she invited him to the launching of their new boat.

"We bought it with a small part of the settlement," she said.

"The Chu Chu Too," she said.

30

When Brandon arrived back at his apartment he saw that the door was ajar. He stood at the threshold and peered down the hallway.

At the end of the hallway he saw the kitchen.

Inside the kitchen he saw his refrigerator.

The refrigerator was sideways. It was tipped on its side.

31

Brandon went to Miranda July's.

He went to Kara's.

He called his mother.

No one was home.

Brandon called the prison in Ohio. He was transferred from the switchboard operator to a prison guard and then was put on hold.

Eventually his father came on the phone.

"Brandon?" said Brandon's father.

"Yes," said Brandon.

He asked his father about prison life.

"Fine," said his father.

He said the food was fine. His bed was fine. His roommate was fine. He liked the rigid schedule. He had lots of time to read.

"The library is very impressive," he said.

He said, "I've read Bentham, Kierkegaard, and Foucault."

Brandon told his father that was happy to hear that he was enjoying his imprisonment.

He said, "After all, the system is designed to do more than punish."

"Indeed," said Brandon's father. "The system is meant to lead to a reconciliation with reality. Crime is the refusal to accept the basic facts of existence. In most rational societies that which is abhorrent to nature is also against the law."

He asked Brandon if he'd heard about the gray whales.

"Take those gray whales for example," his father said. "Their refusal to decay in the ocean is criminal. It goes against their very function in nature. The function of gray whales is to live and decay in the ocean. If they refuse to do the latter who will feed the bottom feeders?"

"Anarchy," said Brandon.

"Exactly," his father said.

32

Numb nose.

Cold nose.

No nose?

33

"You look terrible," said Kara.

"The teenagers," said Brandon.

"Again?"

"I'm afraid to go home."

Brandon explained about his refrigerator.

Kara closed the door and stepped outside her apartment.

She asked where he'd been staying.

"The Saharan Motel," said Brandon. He told her that his room looked out onto the pool. It had a bed, an air conditioner, and a minibar, which technically was more than he had in his own apartment.

He told her that whenever he tried to fall asleep, he'd hear the minibar and be reminded of his own refrigerator.

He hadn't slept in a week.

"Can't you unplug it?" said Kara.

"I tried that," said Brandon.

He told Kara that the maid had found the cord and told the management about it. The management had threatened to kick him out.

"But I have worse problems," said Brandon.

He told Kara that his nose had turned from numb to cold.

"Can you lose a nose?" said Kara.

Brandon didn't know for sure but he thought that you could.

"Oh yes," he said. "You can definitely lose a nose."

34

After they went to the doctor's, Kara drove Brandon back to his motel.

"Now we know," said Kara.

They sat on Brandon's bed and listened to the sound of his minibar's engine. There was a vacuum cleaner in the distance. On the wall was a picture of a slow camel moving toward an oasis.

"Yes," said Brandon.

"I'm relieved," said Kara.

She said, "I'm happy that your nose is fine."

"It's not fine," said Brandon.

"It's broken," he said.

"But you're not going to lose it," said Kara.

"That's true," said Brandon.

She said, "The only type of nose you can lose is a syphilitic nose."

Outside the sun quivered in the swimming pool.

A child sat in the sandbox and built a shapeless lump.

"I don't have syphilis," said Brandon.

He said, "Because I haven't been having sex."

"Promiscuous sex," said Kara.

She said, "You can only get syphilis from having promiscuous sex."

Brandon thought about Charles.

Promiscuous sex, he thought.

35

Everyone gathered at the marina for the launch of the Chu Chu Too.

Brandon was gathered with a fresh bandage across his nose. Kara was gathered. Charles was gathered. Javier was gathered. Miranda July was gathered.

Charles wielded a bottle of champagne.

He held it by its neck, ready to smash it against his brand new yacht.

But before he smashed his champagne he made a speech.

Charles: "Back in the Viking times, the Vikings marked the launch of a new boat with a human sacrifice. They sacrificed a human and spilled his blood into the sea to satisfy the sea gods. Like Vikings we are gathered here today to launch a new boat. But unlike Vikings we are not allowed to sacrifice human beings. Instead we are going to sacrifice a very expensive bottle of champagne. May this bottle of champagne satisfy the sea gods so that they protect us on this voyage and on many voyages to come."

He broke the bottle and everyone applauded.

Kara handed out yachting caps.

Everyone boarded the boat.

36

"How do you like it?" said Miranda July.

"Fun," said Brandon.

"My first time on a boat," he said.

Brandon and Miranda July stood alone at the rear of the boat. Everyone else was at the front of the boat eating shrimp on toothpicks and laughing.

The laughter flew back like spray from the waves.

Brandon's nose was bleeding.

He was cold and nauseous.

Every time the boat bumped over a wave he grabbed the rails and choked down a tide of vomit.

The boat hit a wave and Brandon grabbed the rail.

"I hate boat rides," said Miranda July.

She said, "Boat rides always go on too long. The sun is always too hot. The boats are always too confining. But every time I'm invited, I accept. I think maybe this time it will be different. Maybe this time it will be a fun boat ride. But at the same time I know exactly what's going to happen."

"What's going to happen?" said Brandon.

"Reality," said Miranda July.

37

After they had sailed past Venice Beach and Santa Monica Beach and had begun the long curve up the coast toward Malibu, Charles called everyone to the front of the boat.

He and Javier had brought along golf clubs and wanted everyone to hit golf balls into the sea.

He offered Kara the chance to go first.

"What about the fish?" said Kara.

"What fish?" said Charles.

Kara said, "I don't want to hit a fish."

"You won't hit a fish," said Charles.

He handed a club to Javier and Javier swung it.

The ball landed far away in the water.

There was a tiny, white splash.

"See," said Charles.

"The ocean is vast but mostly fishless," he said.

He gave a club to Miranda July and she dutifully knocked a ball into the water.

Then he gave one to Brandon.

"Let's see if you remember how it goes," said Charles.

Brandon looked out at the ocean.

Then he looked at Kara.

Her nose.

Her brown eyes.

But not her breasts, thought Brandon.

Not her breasts, he thought.

"I can't," said Brandon.

"The fish," he said.

Charles hit two more balls into the water.

"No fish," he said.

"Oh it does look like fun," said Kara.

She stood at the front of the boat and raised the club above her head.

She swung.

But before the club connected with the ball the boat bumped over a wave and everyone lunged forward.

When Brandon stood up again he looked to the spot where Kara had been standing.

Kara was gone.

38

Everyone stood at the rail and called into the water.

But there was no Kara.

There was just blue-black sea.

Charles climbed over the rail and dived into the ocean.

Javier peeled off his shirt and jumped in as well.

Miranda July clutched a lifesaver.

"Look," she said.

She pointed at a floating whale corpse that had surfaced alongside the ship. There was a whole rotten pod of them.

"It's the whales," said Miranda July. "That's what we hit."

Brandon could smell them.

"The stench," he said.

"Truly horrible," said Miranda July.

Then Brandon saw Kara. She was clinging to a whale corpse and drifting further away from the boat.

"There she is," said Brandon.

He climbed up the rail and pointed.

"Kara," he said.

"I'm coming," he said.

But Charles and Javier had also seen her.

They began swimming toward her, their muscular arms pulling them through the water with ease.

By the time Brandon had removed his shirt they had already reached her. The three were hugging together and paddling back toward the boat.

The rescue was already over.

It's too late, he thought.

But Brandon jumped in anyway.

He mounted the rail and plunged into the water.

He was a poor swimmer and was dunked by the waves. But when he got his head above the water he could see Kara and Charles moving together in the distance.

The whales rose and sank around him.

"I'm coming," he said.

There was music in the water, the sound of waves slapping on whales' bodies.

He was moving farther away from the Chu Chu Too but he didn't seem to be getting any closer to Kara and Charles.

"I'm coming," he said. "Wait."

PANIC ATTACK

From: Dan & Nan [editor@------mag.org]
Sent: 18 June 2014
To: K--- J------ [k---@----lit.com]
Subject: RE: Bryan Hurt

Hi K---,

We enjoyed Bryan's story, but we are looking for something more true, something that explores deeper human emotions. Bryan's stories do not have as much emotional depth as I think we are looking for. Might he have something else that is more along these lines?

Hope all is well!
Nan

Nan says that my stories aren't real enough. She and Dan like them, she says, but they want something that's more true. Even the true stories I send them, stories about stuff that really happened, aren't true enough. They want *true* true. The kind of truth that builds a nest in your heart, lays eggs, and two weeks later little baby truth birds hatch out. That's the kind of truth she's talking about. "Truth birds?" I say. "Or bombs," says Dan. "The kind of story where you read it and—" he makes a kaboom gesture with his hands like a bomb blowing up.

"So you want a story with birds or bombs in it?" I say. I'm hunched over my notebook taking notes.

"No!" they say. Birds and bombs are just metaphors. They want stories about real things, stuff with real emotional depth.

"Got it," I say. "No birds, no bombs." I scratch both off my list.

"And no ghosts," says Nan. "No zombies, no spaceships, no time travel, no fairy tales. None of that funny stuff." They want straight-up, regular stories about real-life emotional things. "We believe in you," says Dan. "We know you can do it."

Me, I'm not so sure. I like Nan and Dan a lot and want them to like me back. But the way they're talking about my stories makes me feel like I'm a psychopath. Like I deliberately put a heavy lid over my feelings or that the tap to my emotions is completely shut off. But the tap to my emotions is not shut off. I look down at the floor. While my eyes are down there, I notice that Dan's sneakers are a limited edition. I've never seen them back home in LA. "Thanks," says Dan. He sips his drink, gets mustache in his beer. "They *are* a limited edition. They only sell them here in Williamsburg. You have to be from Brooklyn to buy them. They make you show an ID and everything before you pay." Compared to his shoes, my sneakers are nothing. The black parts are brown, the white parts are black, and there's dog poop dried to the soles.

"We didn't come here to talk about shoes," says Nan. "We're here to talk about stories. What do you say? Do you have the kind of story we're looking for?" I look at the list that I jotted down on the airplane, but after Nan's tirade almost all of my ideas are crossed out:

~~Time travel~~

~~Zombies~~

~~Ghost~~ pirates

"What about pirates?" I say. Of course I know what they'll say pretty much immediately. But I'm not very good at making things up on the spot. Nan lifts her glasses, pinches the bridge of her nose. Dan blinks. A silence, tight as piano wire, stretches across the bar. "Sad pirates," I say. Someone coughs apologetically.

"Well," says Dan. "I like the sad part. That feels true to me. Sadness is real." Nan sighs. "Look," she says. "We're not saying we need a story right away. Think about it. Maybe send us an email when you get home."

When I get home I'm still shivering from the plane ride. I paid twelve dollars for a chicken sandwich that tasted like it was made in a lab. Everyone was too big for their seats. My wife is on the couch, underneath an Indian blanket, reading the Sunday magazine in the *New York Times*. "How'd it go?" she asks. I uncork the wine, pour myself a glass. Upstairs the neighbor's big dog starts scratching. The building is old and everything is thin—the walls, the ceiling. Our ceiling lamp shakes.

"We should move," I say.

"Can't," says my wife. This is true. We could barely afford our place when we moved in three years ago, and we can barely afford it now. But it's rent-controlled. Since the recession, we can't afford anything else.

I'm feeling anxious from the plane ride. I down the wine in two drinks, but still the need to do something is like a rash. "Want to fool around?" I say.

My wife looks at the clock. It's inching toward ten o'clock. "I would," she says. "But I should be in bed already. Need to get up early for a conference call with the East Coast." She yawns. "Tomorrow? Pencil it in?"

I throw myself on the couch, switch on the TV, and flip between channels for a while before settling on a show about science. A famous scientist is talking about global warming, mankind's eventual doom. When I wake it's from a bad dream I don't remember. The TV's off and my wife has gone to bed. I lie there for a while trying to remember the dream and feeling my heart beat. The more I try to remember the dream—the more I can't—the faster my heart beats. It takes a few minutes to realize that I'm having a full-blown panic attack.

I stumble to the kitchen, splash water on my face, pour myself a glass. The apartment might be crappy but you can't complain about the location. Out the window there's a clear view of the ocean. Tonight, the moon's big over the water, fog rolling in. To the north a foghorn's blowing. I drain another glass and focus on my swallowing, like focusing on my swallowing will slow down my pounding heart. When did I start having panic attacks? I'm not that old. I live by the ocean. I have a beautiful wife. What do I have to panic about?

The toilet flushes and my wife walks into the hallway. "Still awake?" she says.

"Can't sleep." All of the sudden my heart moves into my throat. I feel like I'm going to cry.

"Sit with me on the couch," she says. We sit and she holds my hand. "It's going to be okay," she says. She shushes me and wipes a tear off my cheek. "It's going to be okay."

But the more she says it, the less I know for certain. I don't even know what *it* is. What's going to be okay? Are we going to make more money? Be less stuck? Be less tired? Will we have more sex again like we did when we were in our twenties? Back when it seemed like we were more in love?

I want a story that answers yes to all of these questions. A story that's definitely not a real story because it tells me that things will get better. A story that slips past the truth like a pirate at midnight. The story that my wife is telling me while she's patting my hand and smuggling me lies.

HEAVENS

1. You have pain in your back and can't sleep. For three months it goes on like this: back pain, waking up, going to the couch, reading a magazine, not sleeping. Everyone you know asks why you look so tired, why your bad mood. Your wife doesn't ask.

2. You go to the doctor and the doctor puts you in a machine. While the machine takes pictures of your back, it plays classical music. You don't know anything about classical music except that it's depressing. Violins don't cover up the machine's noise, and when they do, it's not like it's enough. No music in the world can hide the fact about where you are at that moment, in the basement of a hospital, inside a tube. Also depressing is the fact that your doctor can't find it. "Your pain," he says, "it's in your head."

3. You go to a psychologist. "Of course it's in your head," the psychologist says. He asks where else you expected your pain to be. He says that the best thing to do is to surrender to it. Try marijuana. "Seriously," he says. "We live in California." He rubs his beard and asks about your mother.

4. You tell your wife that the psychologist says to surrender. "That's not the same as giving up," she says. "Suicide is not surrender."

5. But it's not just back pain that you've been moaning about. It's the shittiness of the world in general. Of course, it's not the world in general that you find so shitty. It's the world as you perceive it vis-à-vis its shittiness

toward you. Your wife says that if you don't stop feeling sorry for yourself, she's going to leave you. She loves you, she says, but it's clear that you're not thinking about her. You tell her that she doesn't mean it. Actually, she says, she does. That night neither of you sleep. You, on the couch, in the meanest part of yourself, in the bile-producing ducts in your gallbladder, and in the empty spaces in between, feel this as a victory.

6. But in the morning she comes out of the bedroom with her suitcase. She's going to stay with her parents. Not forever, she says. But definitely for a couple of nights.

7. You call your mother. You ask how she could have done this to you. "Done what?" she says. Bring you into a world, you say, where everything is turned against you. "You mean a world," she says, "where most of the people you know love you. A world," she says, "where you're considered a contributor to the total sum of good." She asks how she could not.

8. But you go ahead and do it anyway, that thing that you've been threatening to do. You do it in the bathtub with pills. You regret it too almost immediately after you've swallowed them. But by then it's too late. It's true what they say: What's done is done. How sad is that?

9. When you open your eyes you're in a room with your grandmother. She's your grandmother but she's also an angel. You're an angel too. You have the halo and the wings. The room you're in is white and there's harp music playing. It's not, truth be told, all that different from being in an MRI. "That was stupid," your grandmother says. You ask if you're in Heaven. Your grandmother rolls her eyes.

10. You sleep all the time in Heaven. It's practically the only thing to do. When you're not sleeping you play in an orchestra. Because that music in MRI machines? It's not being piped in at all. There are literally orchestras of angels that go to hospitals and play for sick people. In life, you never

had the patience to be a musician, but in Heaven, after you put some effort into it, you find that you have some talent for the violin.

11. When your mother and wife show up in Heaven, they're happy to see you but also kind of surprised. You know, you say. You were surprised too. But Hell's a lie, something that they made up down on Earth. Your wife doesn't believe it. "Not after what you put us through," she says. "It's just different," she says, "different than what we thought it would be." She says that she was sad for a long time. She even thought about suicide herself. But then she met someone new. They got married, had kids. Her new husband is already up there in Heaven. It turns out that you know him. He plays saxophone in your orchestra. You like him. He's a nice guy.

12. And that's the thing about Heaven: eventually everyone you know shows up. For a while it's like Facebook, or a really great party, but then the conversation dies out. Because there are no politics in Heaven; there's no weather. Even the music gets old. You've heard all the harp music a thousand times. You've played all of the violin solos. Why on Earth doesn't anyone write any great violin solos anymore?

13. One day, you go to ask your grandmother what it is that she does to pass the time. But you can't find your grandmother. You check all of the rooms in Heaven and realize that it's not just your grandmother who's missing. Your mother and your wife are gone too. All of the faces are changing. You don't recognize anyone anymore.

14. Back in your room, you sit on your bed and think about all of the people you used to know in Heaven. Your grandmother, your wife. The priest who officiated over your funeral. Your sister. Your sister's twin daughters. The daughters' sons and the sons' daughters. Presidents of the United States, those you voted for and those you did not. Even your wife's new husband, the saxophone player, even he is no longer in Heaven. You

close your eyes and try to sleep, but for the first time since you've come to Heaven, you can't.

16. Soon the phone next to your bed begins ringing. It's an old-fashioned phone, black and with a cord. You pick it up and on the other end is your grandmother. "Listen," she says, "you've enjoyed yourself, right? You've had a good time?" Of course you've had a good time. You've been in Heaven. "Here's the thing," she says. "You can't stay in Heaven forever." Why not? "It's kind of like Disneyland," she says. "They have to keep the lines moving."

17. You wrap the cord around your fingers. You feel like crying. You wonder if they lied to you about this being Heaven, if they lied to you about Hell being a lie. You ask your grandmother where you'll go next. Your grandmother sighs. She says that you'll go to another Heaven, of course, a Heaven where everyone is already waiting for you. A Heaven with rock music, she says, and picnics, with great, big outdoor spaces and lots of dogs. It'll be different from the Heaven you've known, but it's a Heaven all the same. And after that, when the picnic's over and the dogs have gone to sleep under the picnic tables and the ants are carrying away the chicken bones, you'll go to another Heaven. And another Heaven. Because there's always another Heaven. And another Heaven after that.

MOONLESS

It took some doing but I finally made a white dwarf star like they'd been making out in Santa Fe. I made mine in my basement because basements are the perfect place to compress time and space. I slammed together some very high-frequency energy waves and—ZAP!—a perfect miniature white dwarf. Even though it was very small for its type, no larger than a pushpin, it was extremely dense and incredibly bright. The star was so bright that you couldn't look directly at it. Had to look above or below or off to the side and squint. One time I set myself the challenge of just staring at it for thirty seconds. Got a big headache, huge mistake.

Density was a problem too. The star was dense enough that it drew small objects toward it. Tissue paper, curtains, the tail of my cat. Of course they all burst into flames. But at the same time, it wasn't so dense that it just hovered there above my table, an object fixed in space. It wobbled this way and that, wandering the basement, knocking against the walls, the floor, the ceiling, leaving burn marks everywhere. The last straw was when it set fire to my favorite Einstein poster—the one with his tongue sticking out, his messed up hair and goofy grin. I trapped the star in a box, put a padlock on the heavy lid.

But stars are not meant to be kept in boxes. At night I could hear it down in my basement bumping against the walls of its prison. My dreams were soundtracked by a million leaden pings. The only solution was to make another one. A second white dwarf that matched the first one exactly and set both of them into a stable binary orbit. The two stars dancing around their common center of gravity. It was a simple and elegant solution, as most solutions from nature are.

But once I had the stars locked in equilibrium, I couldn't help but notice how shabby the rest of their surroundings were. The basement's dull walls, spiderwebs hanging from the ceiling beams, boxes stacked and packed with old LPs and moth-eaten sweaters and love letters from girlfriends who'd liked me first for my ambition and then called it neglect. So I went to the art store and bought black poster board, which I glued together and strung with Christmas lights. I called the finished product the Universe even though it was more like a diorama of it. Still I felt the display added some dignity to the scene, my white dwarves floating there in front of all that blackness, the holiday lights shining behind. My cat liked it too. He rubbed his cheeks against the sharp corners of the universe and purred.

Exactly when it happened, I don't know. But soon little globes of matter began forming around my stars. The globes were made of drops of water from the glass I'd spilled, Einstein ashes, and fur that the stars pulled from the back of my cat who liked to nap underneath them. There were two of them, two globes. They were more like tiny planets really, each one orbiting its own star. I put my elbows on the table and squinted at them from behind my welder's mask (for by then I'd learned my lesson). One planet was slightly larger than the other, had its own miniature moon, so I named it after a moony ex-girlfriend who liked to stare at the night sky and ask why our love wasn't as dark and infinite. The other one had no moon, so I called it Moonless.

The next time I checked on my cardboard universe, even more had changed. There was a tiny flag planted on the tiny moon. Microscopic satellites orbited the planet and miniature airplanes flew to miniature cities. Each city swarmed with tiny cars with subatomic, red-faced drivers inside. Moonless was doing even better; its civilization had become even more advanced. There were hovercars, biodomes, black glass buildings that swooped and curved as if they'd been painted into existence. On top of its tallest mountain was an enormous telescope that was pointing at its neighbor. Operating the telescope was a tiny scientist in a tiny white lab coat, her hair twisted into a tiny-but-perfect black knot.

But I was not in the right mood to appreciate the wonders of my universe. I could not force myself to feel the requisite joy or awe or whatever I should have felt at that particular moment in time. I had just returned home from my laboratory, it had been a not-so-great day. First I'd been rejected by one of my lab assistants. Not even formally rejected. Asked her out and she just jammed her eyes into a microscope and hummed. Then I'd lost out on a big government grant to my chief rival, the smug molecular astrophysicist, Dr. Hu. I patted him on the back and ate his celebratory cake, forced a smile with icing on my lips. Someone had dented my car in the parking lot. My cat had made a hairball in one of my loafers, which I stepped in as soon as I got home.

So no. I could not muster the enthusiasm to celebrate the triumph of my dwarves, the impossibility of their little people. What I felt instead, primarily, was annoyed.

Because take for example the planet named after the moony ex-girlfriend: here was a brand new world, unlimited potential, infinite possibilities, and it was basically just a smaller copy of this one. Same cars, same space junk, same flag on the moon. Pretty much all the same crap except played out on an even smaller, more insignificant scale. Pathetic, really. Boring. Much like the girlfriend I'd named the planet after. After a promising start—exciting, sexy—it was a movie on the couch every Friday night, maybe with a little petting mixed in. But when I'd start taking her pants off, she'd yawn and say she liked it better in the morning when she was not tired but still half-asleep. As if sex was something that happened only once a day, like breakfast or sunsets. In the end she was the one who said I didn't love her. Said that if I didn't like what she had to offer, I'd never be happy. So I flicked the moony planet into the universe's backdrop, watched it explode against the cardboard and Christmas lights. The explosion was so small that it barely even registered as a blip.

But the tiny scientist on Moonless saw it too. She blinked into her viewfinder, pushed her glasses up the bridge of her nose, then turned the telescope in the opposite direction, a full half-circle, so that when it stopped it was pointing directly up at me. She wrote something in her tiny notebook, her tiny hand trembling. I didn't go back into the basement for a while after that.

But basements can't be avoided forever. When I did return—with a basket of laundry so ripe you could practically see the wafterons rising off it—I saw that the tiny scientist had built a gigantic ray gun. She was taking potshots at my Christmas lights. Zapped a light and tiny glass tinkled onto cardboard. I told her to knock it off. She zapped another one. "Or what?" she said. "You're going to destroy this planet too?" Maybe I was. I told her not to test me. "Oh I'll test you," she said. She wheeled the gun around and fired a shot that skimmed my nose. The second one hit me dead on. It stung a lot. I ducked the next salvo and raised my hand to swipe her planet out of existence. She set her chin, bracing for the blow.

But I was not a destroyer of worlds. Not really. I had destroyed one world, and it was just a very small one. I hadn't even meant to create it. What I'd intended to do was make a star, a modest white dwarf, something beautiful just to see if I could do it. Maybe I'd also wanted to have something to show off to girlfriends when I brought them down to my basement, something that would help get them to hop into my bed. I didn't want to contribute to the grand unhappiness. There was already too much of it in this world. Just today I'd read about a kid in Ohio who shot another kid in school. In Japan, someone had taken a knife into the subway and stabbed five people to death. At work, I'd found Dr. Hu crying alone in a bathroom stall. He had stage-four prostate cancer, inoperable, spreading.

Still, perhaps it was all unavoidable. Maybe whenever you made something—stars, planets, people, whatever—you always made a little sadness, a little death. There was no such thing as pure creation. I told the tiny scientist that I was sorry about the planet but either I was going to destroy it or it was going to be destroyed by something else. That's how it worked: that was science, that was the natural order of all things.

"That's bullshit," she said. She said that I was a coward and a chickenshit. She said that her husband had been on that other planet on an expedition. I had killed him. She asked how I wasn't responsible for that. "Look," I said. "I'll make up for it." I pulled some fur from the back of my cat, dunked it in some water and rolled it into a ball, which I set in orbit around the dwarf.

The ball came undone; it drifted into the star and burned to ash. "Pathetic," she said. She looked at me, disappointed and angry, just like every moony Lindsay or Sarah or Kara or Jen looked at me when something came undone between us. But it was just a little thing, an insignificant thing, barely worth dwelling on because it hardly even existed. A small planet; her husband, a small man.

"I'm sorry," I said, and I guess I was. "But what do you want from me? I can't fix everything. I'm not a god."

Even then I think we both knew that wasn't true, not entirely. For after the tiny scientist grew old and died, and her children died, and her planet's sun died, and everyone died, I continued making new stars. I made white dwarves but also other types because my techniques had become more advanced. Sometimes new planets coalesced around these stars and sometimes the planets made life. I continued to flick away the inferior or disappointing ones, or I'd feed them to my cat. Of those that remained I watched tiny people spread out and inhabit all the corners of my tiny universe, until the universe became too full to contain them and so I'd wipe them all away. Sometimes there were other tiny scientists with very powerful telescopes who would look up and out at me. When they saw me there were always questions about who I was and what I wanted. Was I good or malevolent? Omnipotent or indifferent? A god of death? I was just a man, I'd say to them, just as I'd told the original scientist. But like the original scientist, the more they studied me, the more they watched, the more they became unconvinced. Not because I had power over life and death, destruction and creation—which I did. But because there was only one of me. The god of my own isolation, my own unhappiness. A man with a cat in a basement. What is a god if not alone?

ALL OF THE ARCTIC EXPLORERS

PYTHEAS

First of all Pytheas, Pytheas of Greece.

He was everything that you'd expect from an ancient Greek person. Toga, laurel wreath, all of that.

Everywhere he went, he discovered things.

He discovered the Baltic.

He discovered amber.

He discovered the British Isles and everyone living there. People who painted their faces blue and who traded in tin and who had not yet discovered themselves. When his boat made landfall, Pytheas, the British people said, discovered *them*. And then, when he left the British Isles, sailing north, he discovered more things.

The midnight sun.

Pancake ice.

The relationship between the moon and the tides.

Thule.

Thule, he said, was the paradise at the top of the world. The people there lived on millet. The land had the consistency of jellyfish. "Neither land, properly speaking, nor air, nor sea," he said, "but a mixture of these things like a marine lung."

Marine lungs being what they called jellyfish back then.

Today, of course, we know there is no Thule. Thule might have been Iceland, Greenland, or the Faroe Islands.

Who knows, really, what it might have been.

THE IRISH

Next up were the Irish.

Irish monks.

Significant because the inhabitants of the British Isles are the most prodigious of all the Arctic explorers.

The next most being North Americans.

The next most after them being the Danes, the Swedes, and the Norwegians.

The Irish went to Iceland.

Got on a boat and followed a flock of geese.

FLOKI OF THE RAVENS

Also went to Iceland because of birds.

His sobriquet—of the ravens—because of his having sailed with. He had three ravens that he released when his boat went out past the Outer Hebrides. The first of which circled the boat and, not finding land, landed again on the mast.

Also, the second.

The third raven flew northwest and Floki followed.

They arrived, eventually, at Iceland.

Which he called Snowland because of the snow.

He spent one bad winter there.

Bad because he ate the ravens, his pets.

Also bad because of the monks. Monks and Norsemen being mortal enemies. There was lots of killing between them. Mostly killing by Floki but also, too, killing by the monks who were not entirely pacifists. Which is why, today, we don't know much about either having lived on Iceland. There's nothing left of Floki and little of the monks except for some Irish place names.

The island of Papey, after what the monks called themselves, the Papar.

The island where puffins go to mate.

INGÓLFUR THE ICELANDER

For a long time that's how it went.

People went to Iceland.

People died.

For example, in addition to the monks, Floki's daughter, who one day while riding a horse, fell off and into a creek, and drowned. And so another reason why Floki's winter there was a bad one. But then there was Ingólfur. Ingólfur the Norseman who, because of having raped and pillaged in Norway, was fleeing the Norwegian king.

The king chasing Ingólfur.

Ingólfur chasing a door.

Because that's what Norsemen did back then. When they got into trouble they'd toss a door into the ocean and follow it. The Norse gods would guide the door to safety. Their having a favorable disposition toward doors.

The gods took Ingólfur's door to Iceland and so with it Ingólfur. But because of Iceland's being *Ice*land it wasn't such a safe place. There was, among other things, the ice. And everything that the ice signifies.

Such as starvation.

Such as loneliness.

Such as eternal punishment of the soul. The ice, according to Dante, signifying the ninth and deepest layer of hell, its being furthest away from God's warmth. But where else could Ingólfur, not a Christian anyway, go?

Behind him was the king of Norway.

And plus all of the angry Norwegians.

So on Iceland, on the southwest shore, on the ice, Ingólfur took his boat apart and with boat parts (minus one door) built a hut.

And over time more huts.

Because of the princess whom Ingólfur stole from the king of Norway, the king's daughter, Ingólfur's wife, who bore his children.

The children needing huts.

And then huts for the children's children.

And so on.

And so the founding of Reykjavik.

OTHER ARCTICS (LITERAL)

The Arctic where the devil lives, for example, according to Isaiah, in a house of fire on top of a mountain of ice.

The Arctic with the dragon from which all evil comes. Whose smoke it was that Ezekiel saw in his vision of God. The smoke, Ezekiel said, that was coming from the north from out of the dragon's nose and mouth.

The Arctic where the Wisu live. That tribe of people who came, sometimes, down to Bulgaria and killed the Bulgarians' crops. Their very presence, it's said, having been enough to turn water to ice.

The inhospitable Arctic.

The encroaching Arctic.

The Arctic I'm primarily speaking about.

OTHER ARCTICS (FIGURATIVE)

But also the enticing Arctic.

The Arctic, for example, toward which the Bulgarians would spend three months traveling in order to trade with the Wisu, the very same people who'd have, some months earlier, come down and wreaked havoc on their crops. When the Bulgarians arrived, they'd leave their dogcarts in the Arctic, on the border, overnight, and then return in the morning to find that, sometimes, the Wisu had left them goods to exchange.

Dragons' teeth.

Seal skins.

Whale fat packed in straw.

Other times, though, they'd find that the Wisu had killed their dogs and left them nothing. They took it as a sign of displeasure, perhaps.

Or perhaps not.

If not displeasure it was certainly a sign of something.

On the ice, dogs' blood being so visible for so many miles out.

MORE EXPLORERS

Everyone you'd expect went to the Arctic, but also others you might not.

Arabs, for example.

Such as the writer Shams ad-dîn Abû 'Abdallâh Muhammad ad-Dimashqî. And the geographer, Zakariya al-Qazwini, who was Persian, not Arab. But still.

What struck both of them about the Arctic, most of all, was the cold. And the emptiness.

The writer, ad-Dimashqî, said that it was emptiness like _____.

AND COLD

Like a thousand bee stings.

Like a lion's roar.

Cold, ad-Dimashqî said, just as others have said both before and after him, that was inversely proportionate to the heat put out by the fires of hell.

But in the Arctic, for the people who live there, hell and fires are not such easy ideas to understand. The natives thinking that a hot eternity didn't sound like such a bad thing.

Because what's so bad about a fire that never goes out?

MISSIONARIES

Not that this has ever stopped anyone, missionaries in particular, from going north and trying to teach them differently.

For example, and especially, Isaac O. Stringer, the Canadian bishop who wanted to teach the Arctic Inuits about hot hell and Jesus Christ. He who became better known as the bishop who ate his boots because of one day, after trying and failing to convert the Inuits to Anglicanism, his walking home and being caught in a surprise snowstorm.

Snow coming down like *surprise!*

Not that it was a surprise, not really, not to the Inuits who actually lived there, because in the Arctic, in reality, snowing being what it does.

Then, of course, there was the bishop's getting lost.

The food situation.

His having run out.

From the bishop's journal, October 21:
Breakfast of sealskin boots, soles and tops broiled and toasted.
Soles better than tops.

BOOT-EATERS

In the historical sense, boots are a popular source of food for people who have nothing else. For men, in particular. For sad men most of all.

The saddest boot-eater probably being John Franklin.

Not that it's a contest.

Not that anyone's keeping count.

Franklin who was better known as *Sir* John Franklin of the Queen's Royal Navy, his having been knighted for surviving a bad winter up in the Arctic. Sir Boot-Eater to those who knew (everyone) what he'd done.

On Arctic expeditions food is always the first thing to run out.

The second is common decency.

The third is the rule of law.

So Franklin, in the Arctic, lost on the ice, cooked his boots. He wrote a letter to his wife, indecent because of the things he said they'd do together when he returned to London, the types of food they'd eat in bed. Then he killed a guy, a member of his own expedition, whom he suspected of hoarding food.

The sound of the killing attracted polar bears, which Franklin also shot with his rifle. The polar bear meat, in addition to boot leather, being what kept him alive for so many months.

Not that it mattered in the end: his boot-eating, being rescued, or anything else. Because by the time Franklin returned home, his wife, Sweet Jane, had already left him.

She'd run away to Tasmania with a scientist, Franklin's friend.

The scientist, she said, was the only man who could make her swoon.

Then Franklin went on another Arctic expedition, this time looking for the Northwest Passage.

At least that's what he said.

I think he went because he was lonely.

That was the expedition that everyone calls ill-fated.

The way all of its people disappeared.

RESCUE MISSIONS

Usually a bad idea but sometimes not.

For a long time in Europe and North America, when an expedition disappeared, it was *de rigueur* to send out a second.

And then, when the second disappeared, to send out a third.

For a while, in fact, the Arctic was crowded with expeditions getting lost looking for lost expeditions. Rescuers rescuing rescuers.

And sometimes one rescuer, who was cooking his boots, writing a letter to his love back home, would hear a gunshot or smell smoke and find another rescuer, also cooking his boots, also writing a letter, just a mile or two away, through the fog and across the ice.

This is what happened to Fridtjof Nansen, for example.

Nansen the Norwegian who was trying to reach the North Pole first by boat and then by dogsled, his boat having been crushed by the ice.

Nansen who got caught out on the ice by the winter.

Who shot his dogs for food.

Who built a kayak and tried to paddle back home.

But then the walrus attack.

The walrus attacking Nansen's kayak.

Nansen who shot the walrus and ate it and, while repairing his kayak, heard dog barks and voices in the distance.

And then the appearance of Frederick Jackson.

Jackson who'd been sent to look for Nansen. But who'd also gotten lost and had been wandering around the Arctic all winter on the ice.

JACKSON: Have you seen a ship here?

NANSEN: No, my ship is not here.

JACKSON: Aren't you Nansen?

NANSEN: Yes, I am.

REASONS FOR GOING

Financial reasons, mostly.

The Northwest Passage.

The North Pole.

But also, of course, fame and posterity.

The desire to be known.

FAILURES

After Nansen's attempt, there was Andrée's.

Andrée the Swede with the hydrogen balloon. The balloon that was ninety-seven feet tall, weighed a ton and a half, and was assembled in Paris.

That was made of gray and brown varnished silk.

The idea was to fly the balloon to the pole, land, and take pictures. To go above the ice, not over or across it. The ice's shifting, its impermanence, its very iciness being the thing that kills.

But when they found him, many years later, frozen and buried in the ice on White Island, his head separated from the body and his bones picked over, it was a clear reminder that ice isn't the only thing that kills.

Polar bears kill.

Exposure kills.

So does reckless optimism.

Among Andrée's things were a black three-piece suit and a top hat. And in his journal was his plan, upon reaching the pole, to continue flying the balloon to San Francisco, which he estimated to be the closest major city. When he landed he'd put on the suit and walk into the heart of it.

The people would greet him with a parade.

PARADES

And so I think the main reason for going.

Not for literal parades, per se, though also, kind of for literal parades (because, you know, who doesn't want a parade), but for the recognition of having gone somewhere. Parades being thrown to celebrate the end of an absence. Their being a way of saying welcome back.

So that when I return you can say I've missed you.

By Jove, you can say, it's good to see you again.

Until the next time, that is, when the Arctic starts pulling.

Then I'll return to that wild, white loneliness.

That necessary Arctic.

The Arctic that precipitates ticker tape and the thawing of our hearts.

THE LAST WORD

He is mad at her because he says that she says that he always needs the last word.

Which isn't true.

Not true.

Not true at all.

You're doing it, she says. Just now. With all that truth business.

What, he says, following her out of the kitchen and into the TV room.

It, she says.

It what, he says.

Ugh, she says. She picks up the remote and throws it at him. A bad throw because he steps out of the way.

It cracks, the remote and, really, he can't understand it, whatever the it that she's so mad about is. They had been fighting in the kitchen about what? Some kitchen thing. Cooking maybe. Though possibly cleaning. Though possibly neither. Who knows because now they're fighting about something else. The is-ness of this fight canceling out the was-ness of the last one. As when one channel flips to another channel. As when you walk into the TV room and change the channel from a cooking show to a police show, because cooking shows are boring and it's a mystery how anyone—she—could insist on liking them.

Cooking shows have order, she says. Cooking shows have laws.

She continues moving away from him. She moves into the bedroom, then out of the bedroom, then into the bathroom. She sits on the toilet.

Pulling her hair because he is standing in the doorway, blocking the doorway, talking, wanting her to talk about it.

Stop it, she says.

Stop what, he says-kind-of-shouts.

Talking, she says.

But we're fighting, he says.

Yes, she says. Exactly, exactly. Fighting, she says, is a type of silence. By which she means rhetorical silence. Thus literal silence is, rhetorically speaking, the purest way to fight.

But we need to talk about it, he says. Talk about our fighting so that we understand what we're fighting about.

With her free hand, the hand not pulling her hair, she reaches onto the sink and grabs a hairbrush. This time a better throw.

Listen, he says. He's rubbing the hit-by-the-brush spot on his forehead. Soon it will bruise. Maybe, he says, if you stop throwing and start talking. Talk, he says, about what you're so upset about.

Her hand is wishing for something else to throw at him. If only it could throw itself. But no. Nothing to throw. His fault for cleaning the bathroom. So she bites it—her hand—bites it because she's read somewhere about the transporting power of pain.

She lets the pain transport her to the ocean, which is warm and blue and surrounding an island of sand. She swims to the island. Lies in the sand. The quiet and warmth. A seabird comes, squawking, lands in the tree. No squawking, she says. She hurls a coconut. It misses but the seabird flies away.

Not that she's the only one who can do this, transport herself vis-à-vis the power of pain. He's not going to let her. He bites his hand: ocean, island, sand.

She's on the beach, eyes closed, smiling, soaking up sun. Still she senses him. His shadow, the darkness in the darkness, blocking her heat.

Listen, he says. Talk, he says.

No way, she says. She bites her hand and she's on another island.

He bites his hand.

She sees him splashing down into the ocean. His words crashing across the water, him crawling to shore.

She bites her hand, draws blood.

A church. Cool and cavernous, full of colors: reds, oranges, purples, yellows, the stories of the stained glass. It's quiet-like. Well. Like a church. She sits on a bench and admires the stonework. The flying buttresses. The goldwork on the altar. The silent Jesus. The sorrow twisted on his face.

Christ, he says. A church, he says. Thought you hated churches. His hand throbs from all the biting. He plunges it into the cooling font.

I like churches, she says. Not that you've ever asked.

I like churches too, he says. I like the history and the architecture. I like churches more. He walks to the narthex. Appraises a statue, a discalceate, unsmiling saint.

Then the sound of teeth on handflesh. Turns around. She's gone.

After the church, there's a cabin. After the cabin, a mountaintop. After the mountaintop, a hole.

Talk about it, he says. Both of them in the hole, the dirt crumbling around them.

After the hole, there's a deeper hole.

You're making it worse, she says.

But the right words, he says. The right words to make it right.

Then to an even deeper hole. Then a smaller hole. Then a deeper and smaller hole. A hole where there's room enough for only her. A hole that's plugged on top.

He stands at the top of the hole in the needles under the pine trees, calling down into it, into the dirt. I know you can hear me, he says. Then as a question: Hear me, he says. Can you? No?

Back at home in the TV room he watches TV, a cooking show because he can't change the channel because of the remote. He tells himself things. Things like she'll come back to him. She'll come back to him and they'll smile and laugh about this fight, whatever it was about, because by then they'll have forgotten about it, mostly, and he'll have thought of the right words to say to her, the perfect combination of words, words like bandages, like wallpaper, words that patch, that canvas, that erase, that reconcile, that bridge, that bind, the words, the words, the words, because there are so many of them, and there have got to be some that he can say to her. The right words, the words that will make all of this all right.

And down in her hole, in the dirt, after the echo of his last word has faded, she enjoys her silence. Because it's in that silence that new words grow. Change is a word that she can feel growing. Different is another one. Maybe even alone.

CONTRACT

1.1   When the CEO took his children to the bone altar, the girl turned her head and exposed the softest part of her neck. She was ready for it.

1.2   She knew that all fathers sacrificed their daughters eventually, so didn't protest much when the knife went in.

1.3   The boy resisted. Bit at the CEO's fingers, thrashed, and screamed. Betrayal showed in his eyes long after expression had left the rest of his body. Blood seeped from the line that the CEO had drawn on his neck.

1.4   What else could the CEO do?

1.5   He'd already sacrificed the dog, the cat, the guinea pig, the goldfish. He'd sacrificed his personal assistant, which was sad because she gave really good blowjobs. So in a sense, he'd sacrificed those too. He'd made all of his vice presidents sacrifice their families and then he sacrificed his vice presidents. Everyone who worked for the CEO sacrificed and was sacrificed on his altar of bone.

1.6   But it wasn't enough.

1.7   It was never enough. Every three months, the CEO had new quarterly profits to report, investors to satisfy. He put his knife in his belt and drove to his home by the ocean. Washed his children's blood from his hands and watched it rinse down the sink, through the pipes that would deposit it into the water below.

1.8   His wife asked how it went.

1.9   Next time it will be you, he said. I have nothing else to sacrifice.

1.10   I see, she said. She was not surprised. She'd always expected this, her turn in the sacrifice.

2.1   Her own father had been a CEO. She'd seen her mother's blood on his sacrificial knife, her mother's body slung over his bone altar.

2.2   She herself had escaped the sacrifice once already, escaped first by going away to boarding school in Switzerland. In Switzerland, there were cows and cowbells and endless fields of bluebells and buttercups. There were no CEOs in Switzerland. At least not until her father showed up on graduation day to complete the sacrifice.

2.3   Sacrifice a cow, she'd said. Sacrifice my roommate.

2.4   She pushed a slim French girl toward her father.

2.5   For four years the French girl had clipped her toenails off the top bunk so that sometimes the CEO's daughter found them in her bed sheets or in her socks or worse between her own toes when she forgot and walked around the room barefoot.

2.6   The CEO shook his head. That wasn't how the sacrifice worked. It had to cost him something in order to be meaningful.

2.7   What about the bone altar? said the daughter.

2.8   The CEO said that he'd chosen her boarding school specifically be-
       cause of its proximity to bone altars. There was a church in the town
       across the lake, he said, with an altar of skulls.

2.9   Each skull bleached and wearing a crown of edelweiss.

2.10   There's nothing to be done, said the CEO.

3.1   So the daughter sacrificed herself. She took her father's knife from
       her father's belt and hacked off her own left hand.

3.2   It took three hard hacks for the hand to come off.

3.3   Then, still bleeding, she paddled a boat across the lake to the boys'
       school where she slept with the cricket team. She slept with the
       chess club and Model United Nations.

3.4   She rode out of town on the back of a motorcycle, helmetless, stump
       wrapped in cotton, but still bleeding through.

3.5   She smoked unfiltered cigarettes, snorted cocaine off the plump
       butts of prostitutes. She got a hook for her stump, got syphilis, got
       antibiotics, got pregnant, got an abortion.

3.6   Each time she was arrested for shoplifting or smashing a lover with
       a wine bottle or setting fire to the curtains or tossing a coffee table
       through the hotel window, she said that she was the CEO's daugh-
       ter. She gave her father's full name, spelled it out, so that when
       the arrest was reported in the *Financial Times* or the *Wall Street
       Journal*, her father had to issue a press statement denying any sort
       of connection.

3.7   I have no hook-handed daughter, he'd say. We are not related.

3.8 He was never able to satisfy investors who knew all about perception and the bottom line.

3.9 Then he died of CEO's disease.

3.10 A heart attack.

4.1 On that day his daughter went to the prosthetist's and replaced her hook-hand with a more hand-like hand. Went to the jeweler's and bought a ring for her new plastic ring finger.

4.2 The ring was white gold with a yellow diamond.

4.3 The diamond was almost the same yellow as the yellow in the edelweiss crowns that sat on the skulls in the skull altar in Switzerland.

4.4 It served to remind the CEO's daughter of the reach of fathers.

4.5 She liked to stand in front of mirrors, hold the ring next to her face and admire the way that the diamond nearly matched the yellow ribbons that were threaded through the browns of her eyes.

4.6 It was because of her eyes that she caught the CEO's attention.

4.7 Not her father the CEO, the other one. The CEO who would become her husband.

4.8 Every day he came to the coffee shop where she worked as a foam artist, making milk swans and hearts and flowers on the tops of macchiatos and lattes.

4.9 Every day he ordered a black coffee.

4.10　And admired her eyes, the sadness that lived deep in the bottoms of them.

5.1　All CEOs are experts in loss so he recognized hers instantly. Saw her father drama in the yellow threads, her sorrow and sacrifice. He knew that she'd given up much and so had profited tremendously. As a CEO he wanted to share in her profits, to possess them.

5.2　He left notes for her in the tip jar folded inside brand new twenty-dollar bills.

5.3　I like your eyes more than money.

5.4　I'd sacrifice my mother for a chance to hold your hand.

5.5　One day he did. Brought his mother's bloody head and dropped it next to the tip jar.

5.6　The head oozed on the counter; its stump on the countertop made a sucking sound.

5.7　My mother's head, he said.

5.8　What could the CEO's daughter do? She knew the rules, understood the CEO's sacrifice. The head wobbled and she considered its expression. Not surprise so much as resignation. Like the mother knew, had always known, exactly what was going to happen.

5.9　All sons sacrifice their mothers eventually.

5.10　The CEO's daughter tapped her hand on the counter so he could hear the plastic thump. My hand's a prosthetic, she said. He said it didn't matter. He'd hold it anyway.

6.1   At the French restaurant he did.

6.2   In the candlelight, which reflected off the brushed silver of knives and forks and spoons, he held her hand across the table, their hands snaked between champagne flutes and small plates: warm Camembert, trout tartare, wild mushroom fricassee.

6.3   He held her hand while a French singer sang "La Vie en Rose." He rubbed her ring, caressed her plastic ring finger, told her that she was beautiful.

6.4   For her part, the CEO's daughter didn't want to fall in love with the CEO.

6.5   Did not want to.

6.6   After all, she'd sacrificed her hand to be free from one CEO. Why should she sacrifice her freedom to be with another?

6.7   But when she looked across the table and saw the bruises on his lips, the scratches on his cheeks, the blood that had crusted in the corners of his nose, she knew that his mother hadn't died easily.

6.8   His sacrifice had cost him a lot of effort.

6.9   When was the last time that someone had worked so hard for her?

6.10 It was back at the boarding school in Switzerland. Her roommate, the French girl. They'd kissed a little, the roommate and the CEO's daughter. It was just making out, the CEO's daughter would tell herself as the roommate vacuumed her toenails, let the CEO's daughter copy her chemistry homework. The roommate went down to the cafeteria to bring back breakfast for two, omelettes with goat cheese, sausage, and spinach. Maybe she would skip class, the CEO's daughter thought as she lay in bed, waiting for breakfast and watching dust float in the sun slants. She would skip class and copy her roommate's notes and then they would kiss some more. They were young and there was no harm in being young and kissing.

7.1   Then the CEO asked her to marry him.

7.2   This was not a surprise.

7.3   She saw it coming from a hundred miles away.

7.4   After the horse riding in the park, the picnics at Point Dume, the wine tasting. After the dinner parties with his CEO friends, yacht trips, a vacation in the Bahamas. After the candlelit dinners alone at his house, dinners he'd cooked for her. I'm sorry I'm not a better cook, he said. Which wasn't true, a humblebrag. He'd studied in Provence. Made her coq au vin. The chicken steamed in wine, seared in fat. I just wish I were a better cook, he said again, without modesty. He added blood to the sauce, for thickening.

7.5   They were sucking meat from the bones when he asked the question. She tried to act surprised, but she was not surprised. As unsurprised as the CEO's mother.

7.6   She did not want to marry her father.

7.7   She told her therapist this, who said that this was a common concern, something that many people worried about, so was perfectly normal.

7.8   But who cares, said her therapist. Marry your father or anyone else you want to marry. It doesn't matter so long as you're happy.

7.9   So father-fear aside, she married the CEO. Married him because even though he was a CEO, she liked everything he did for her, liked the way he held her hand and looked into her eyes, liked that he used blood to thicken the sauce, liked the way he made her feel. Which was valued, loved, and happy.

7.10 They honeymooned in Hawaii.

8.1   It was in Hawaii while they sat on a bluff of volcanic rock and watched the sun set into the ocean that the CEO sacrificed his cell phone.

8.2   Tossed the phone into the water and promised that for a week he wouldn't answer to shareholders or boards of directors. Instead, he said, he'd answer to her alone, be her CEO completely.

8.3   But on the drive back to the resort hotel, a seagull flew into their windshield.

8.4   It flopped off the windshield and onto the road where it landed on the yellow line, flapping.

8.5   And at the hotel the concierge met them with message slips, said that since sunset the CEO's room phone hadn't stopped ringing.

8.6   A dead bird was an accident. But a dead bird and phone messages, said the CEO, that was an omen.

8.7   In their room the CEO turned on the flat-screen and saw a plummeting red line. His stock was down, and dropping. He paced the room from bathroom to balcony, muttering. Mutter, he said. Mutter, mutter.

8.8 It had been a mistake, a miscalculation. A CEO is not free. He cannot give his heart away, cannot toss his cell phone, cannot do whatever he pleases. There are always shareholders everywhere. Ubiquitous shareholders. For all he knew the concierge was a shareholder. He could be in the lobby right now selling his shares, reporting on the CEO to his board of directors.

8.9 The CEO fumbled for the knife in his belt. Apologies, he said to his new wife. But you understand how it works, he said. My sincerest apologies. Sorry.

8.10 She did understand, was not naïve. After all, she'd survived her father. Had the ring and plastic hand to prove it. But she had not expected it to come so early in their marriage. Still, while he fumbled for his knife she reached for hers, the one she'd hidden in her suitcase between the lingerie and bikinis.

9.1 A standoff.

9.2 Knives to necks. Pinch, pinch, blood, blood. One red line and then another.

9.3 When he applied pressure, she applied the same amount of pressure back. When he twisted the tip of his knife, she twisted hers.

9.4 Not that anyone got killed. You know that. Not here in this hotel room, obviously. Because the story has made certain promises to its readers. Obligations. Children that will be murdered some years later. Another standoff, similar to this one but in a kitchen with marble countertops and stainless steel appliances. The blood of his children still wet on the CEO's knife, drying.

9.5   So you know all about the knock on the door. The concierge with the silver platter. Did someone order room service?

9.6   Room service? The CEO moved his knife away from his wife's neck. His wife kept hers steady. Ha ha, he said. It's not what it looks like.

9.7   The concierge did not care what it looked like.

9.8   He had seen everything.

9.9   For example, the orgy that was happening two floors above them. If you really wanted to see something, then you should have been paying attention to the orgy. That, he thought. That was something.

9.10 He hoped for a tip but did not expect one. He asked: Where should I put the platter?

10.1 Upstairs at the orgy, bodies slipped between bodies, humping, kissing, all tongues and sex parts and fingers. The CEO's wife joined in. Her body moving with the bodies. Her mouth meeting mouths, fingers touching soft flesh. Hot breath, humid breathing.

10.2 As far as orgies went, it was an okay orgy. Conventional with blindfolds and handcuffs and satin. She had been in better. The chess club orgy in Switzerland, for example. The cocaine orgies in Paris.

10.3 But she enjoyed the human contact. Human contract. The promise of bodies.

10.4 As when two sets of lips meet on a Tuesday morning in bed in Lausanne, two mouths meeting and the brains behind the mouths ignoring the fact that across the quad, class is happening. Or when two hands hold each other on a white linen tablecloth in a dimly lit restaurant, one hand cold and the other hand plastic. Or when the hand with the knife meets the wrist of the hand without. Or when the hand meets the knife and the knife meets the neck and the neck meets the blood and the blood thickens the sauce and the sauce meets the lips and escapes, is ingested.

10.5   Human contract.

10.6   When flesh makes an agreement with flesh, enters into something indissoluble, binding.

10.7   Contract: to make or become smaller.

10.8   A state of being contracted.

10.9   As when the concierge puts the platter on the bed because he has to, it's his job, and waits a moment for the tip he knows will not be coming. Or when the CEO steadies his hand and lifts the lid and his hope for a coq au vin, steamed mussels, or fresh strawberries vanishes. Under the lid is a yellow ring that matches the yellow ribbons in the wife's eyes. A reminder of the story's contract. She will die, she will die. He will kill her.

ROSE

Here's a secret:

It wasn't until after she married the Prince that Briar Rose found out that he had a thing for dead chicks. Now, before you imagine her disappointment, imagine his. His friends didn't tell him that the girl behind all those brambles would still be alive. I bet they laughed pretty hard while he set out to cut and cut away for his dead beauty, only to revive her with a kiss.

Still, they gave it a shot, the Prince and Briar Rose. It really was some kiss. I don't know how it is for you, and maybe it's different for everyone, but for me, when I fall in love, it's a lot like waking up. That's how it was for Briar Rose, too. She'd been asleep for a long time and when the Prince came around and woke her up, she found herself head-over-heels. It wasn't long after that she asked the Prince to marry.

At first, everything was pretty cool. The Prince was upfront about his preferences for the deceased and Briar Rose didn't mind role-playing a bit. There were even some things she liked: erotic asphyxiation, for example. But soon all the Prince wanted to do was do it with her inside of her old glass coffin. "It'll be hot," he coaxed. "Think about it. Your skin, cool glass." But really, after a hundred years squished inside that coffin, there was nothing hot about getting back inside.

One thing to know about the Prince is that he's smaller than he looks on TV. He has small, delicate hands. His feet don't reach the end of the coffin. He stands on a milk crate behind his podium when he gives a speech. He has a tiny penis. "Don't make a sound," he told Briar Rose.

"Don't move a muscle." He wanted her to pretend like she was dead, but really, she didn't have to pretend too hard. When he put himself inside her, he came in about a second. Then he fell asleep right there, right on top. Briar Rose's legs cramped. The Prince's penis shriveled.

The coffin was made of black reflective glass, like the kind they hide security cameras behind at the airport or at the mall. For all the years she slept inside, Briar Rose never spent much time considering her trembling reflection, which cast all around. But under the Prince there was nothing else for her to do. All she could see, all there was, was herself and a cold black expanse. It was depressing to say the least.

And then his whole castle began to feel like a little black box. The garden, the kitchen, her bedroom, the game room with its pinball machines and billiard tables. Everywhere Briar Rose went she felt equally trapped. The Prince wasn't a bad guy but he was dull, his desires repetitive. She started taking other men to bed while he was away fulfilling his princely duties. The gardener, the pool guy, the baker. To bed! To spread out wide across quilted sheets and not be kept crammed in some old sleep-smelling box.

Soon Briar Rose developed something serious with the Prince's steward, a dark-haired guy about a hundred years her junior. It was love, like waking up, and it was an easy secret to keep. The Steward kept the Prince's schedule and knew where he was supposed to be every hour of the day. When the Prince was meeting with foreign dignitaries, they would do it up in his bedroom. And when the Prince was out hunting foxes, they'd bang each other in the stables. Once they even did it on the throne while the Prince was having tea with his mother. And the other castle employees—even if they saw them kissing down in the dungeon—they didn't dare say anything. Briar Rose was queen and could have them hung as easily as fired. So it was a terrible shock when it all ended so badly, with the Steward's death.

The police drained the moat, found the murder weapon—the Prince's gun. They came to arrest him, and the Prince went easily. He walked across the drawbridge, and into the mob of reporters. "No comment," he said again and again and ducked inside the back of a cruiser.

I remember seeing it all on television even though I was just a kid. If you looked carefully you could see Briar Rose there in the background. She was standing in the window up in her tower. You couldn't see her face, but I bet if you could you'd see that she was crying. The Prince didn't look sorry, not once, not even when they called him up on the stand to testify. He stood there impassively and confessed to the murder. "I did it," he said. He said he would have done it a thousand times more. That's how much he loved Briar Rose.

When I met her it was in Boise at the Annual Conference for Museum Curators. By then she was working for the Getty, and had long since dropped Briar from her name. I was sitting on a restoration panel and afterward she introduced herself. We went for drinks and talked about that kouros, the one that made all that news a few years back for being a fake. I asked her about the Prince, and what he was like in real life. Rose was forthcoming. "Small," she said. "A tiny man." Even when they showed him on TV that last time, he in his orange prison jumpsuit, his hands shackled behind his back. Even framed inside the little television box, he looked bigger than he actually was.

She said he still sent her letters. He promised that when he got out of the slammer he'd find her again. "Sometimes he says he loves me," she said. "Sometimes he wants to kill me." She takes pills to fall asleep, that's how nervous the Prince has made her even after all these years. "How terrible," I said. She agreed, and I ordered us another round of drinks.

Still, when I had her in my bed, Briar Rose's hair spread out like sunrays atop the sheets, I could see where the Prince was coming from. I stroked her arms and watched her sleep.

I thought: How pretty she must have looked kept inside a glass box.

THE SADNESS OF TYCHO BRAHE'S MOOSE

1. TRUE STORY

So first of all not a moose exactly.

An elk.

But what an elk.

Moose-like in its magnificence. Nine tines to the antler. Sixteen hands tall at the withers. Bugling voice bright as a trumpet.

The finest elk in all of Denmark.

Loyal as a dog, it followed the astronomer almost everywhere he went.

2. AB OVO

Morning in Denk.

Pale blue sky, clouds like raw wool, bees hovering in the breeze. There amongst the acres of farmland, above a tiny village, sits a brick castle on top of a hill.

Inside the castle, Otte Brahe wakes up next to his wife, Beate Bille.

He smells the air around him.

Rosemary, flowering wheat.

Otte Brahe looks at his wife. He admires her long flaxen hair. The way she's wrapped seductively in the sheets.

He leans over and kisses the mole on her neck.

Beate Bille sighs.

Otte Brahe sighs.

They sigh.

Far above, Mars moves in trine with Jupiter. Five planets in the eastern hemisphere signify a boy.

3. KIDNAPPED

Two years pass.

Tycho Brahe sits in the grass with a tabor drum between his legs. He beats the drum with a single drumstick and harasses an old cow.

The cow stands in a strip of shadow beneath the castle's walls.

Cow looks at Tycho.

Chews grass.

While Tycho beats his drum, Uncle Jørgen storms out of the castle. Uncle Jørgen is Otte Brahe's older brother. He's visiting from southern Denmark, where he's ruler of Vordingborg Castle and sheriff to the king.

Uncle Jørgen slams the door.

He mutters something about a promise.

Otte's promise.

Marches past Tycho and toward the stable and his horse.

Then he stops.

Turns around and looks at his nephew.

Says: "Ach!"

Uncle Jørgen picks up Tycho and throws him on his saddle.

They gallop away.

4. LATER

Later, Otte Brahe and Beate Bille find the drum and the drumstick. There's the same old cow standing in the castle's shadows, still chewing grass.

It's not hard to piece together what must have happened. Otte Brahe tells his wife that they'll let Uncle Jørgen keep Tycho. After all, Uncle Jørgen and his wife are childless; Otte Brahe and Beate Bille, on the other hand, have plenty of children. With the recent arrival of Steen, they have four in all.

And Otte Brahe *did* promise Tycho to Uncle Jørgen eventually, once another son was born. So all things considered, says Otte Brahe, it's not like Uncle Jørgen *stole* the boy. Not exactly.

"Still," says Otte Brahe.

He rubs his beard and looks at the sky. There are honey buzzards circling the castle, cirrus clouds.

He tells Beate Bille that he feels foolish. He says that he really shouldn't have gotten drunk and promised Uncle Jørgen their firstborn son.

5. TYCHO'S MOOSE

Ten years later.

Tycho Brahe is home from the University of Copenhagen.

Winter break.

Since the kidnapping—the *transfer* is what Otte Brahe and Uncle Jørgen now call it—home is with Uncle Jørgen and Aunt Inger on the island of Zealand.

Tycho sits on the back of a horse.

Cold wind blows off the water.

Waves ice the sea.

Tycho lifts his face and feels the stinging pellets of snow blast through the pine trees. In the distance, he sees Goose Tower. Its golden goose weathervane glints under the dull gray sky.

"Papa," says Tycho.

He points to a cow elk grazing in a nearby copse.

Uncle Jørgen exhales a cloud of breath.

He raises his musket.

Cocks the flintlock.

Shoots.

The cow elk staggers and falls into a shrub.

While Uncle Jørgen dresses the elk, Tycho wanders further into the grove. He hears bleating from nearby bog-rosemary bushes. He pulls back the branches and finds a small shivering calf.

Big watery calf-eyes.

Ribs showing through its coat.

Tycho removes his jacket and wraps it around the small animal. He returns with it to his uncle. "Moose," he says.

Uncle Jørgen looks from the baby elk to his nephew and back again. Doting and permissive, he doesn't correct.

6. THE WONDERS OF THE UNIVERSE

Everywhere he goes, Tycho talks about his moose. At school he talks to anyone who'll listen. He tells his teachers and classmates that the moose is kept in the stables with the horses but that during the winter it's allowed to sleep inside next to the fire. He tells them that even Aunt Inger is fond of the animal. She decorates it with bows.

He's telling this to his law professor. He has the professor pinned against a column in the courtyard. Long columnar shadows are splayed across the ground.

Tycho tells his professor that the moose prefers apples to gooseberries; it likes redcurrants best of all.

The professor interrupts. He cranes his neck to look at the sundial in the center of the plaza. He tells Tycho that he must go.

But before the professor can hurry away, the courtyard is cast into sudden darkness. Like a curtain at a playhouse, the moon slides in front of the sun.

The professor stops.

Tycho stops.

Everyone stops.

Where there was once sun, now there is no sun.

A big, blacked-out O.

Some fall to their knees.

Others run for shelter.

The professor swoons.

A solar corona blooms behind the moon's shadow.

Stars appear, thick and white as pennycress.

Tycho gazes at the sky above him.

Most wonderful thing he's seen.

7. FREDERICK II OF DENMARK SAVED FROM DROWNING

Five more years pass, not without significance.

The solar eclipse indicates new beginnings, the sun's steadiness overruled by lunar passions.

Tycho buys an ephemeris based on Copernicus's theories. He buys books by Johannes de Sacrobosco, Petrus Apianus, and Regiomontanus. He learns that his eclipse had been predicted by Ptolemy, that it was part of the same eclipse cycle that blacked out the sun when Christ was on the cross.

But he keeps all this information a secret. He doesn't tell anyone that he's been studying astronomy, not even his tutor. He only whispers it to the moose.

Because science is a fine course of study for alchemists and apothecaries, for middle-class barbers' sons. But Otte Brahe is a member of the Rigsraad. Uncle Jørgen is Vice Admiral of the Danish fleet.

During summer, Tycho smuggles a small celestial globe back home to Vordingborg. He stays up until dawn memorizing the shapes of the constellations.

Orion's belt, the bend of Sagittarius's bow.

When Uncle Jørgen asks him why he's so tired-looking, Tycho lies and tells him that he was up late studying the Edict of Amboise. When Otte Brahe writes and asks how he likes studying court politics, Tycho writes back: *I like them fine.*

But for Tycho, meals with Uncle Jørgen and Aunt Inger are the hardest things to endure. Uncle Jørgen only talks about the latest naval skirmishes with Sweden. Aunt Inger still wants to know more about the latest fashions in Copenhagen.

Tycho forks squab into his mouth and tells her all of the ladies are wearing sable pelts. Rich ladies dip the paws in silver. Jewels replace the eyes.

What Tycho really wants to talk about are the problems with the universe. Lately he's noticed that none of his ephemerides match any of the others. Copernicus's date for the conjunction of Jupiter is a whole month off from that in the *Alfonsine Tables*. Apianus and Regiomontanus have completely different ideas about the location of Mars.

More than anything else, Tycho wants to return to the university and spend long hours in the library poring over star charts, correcting the universe and resetting the stars.

The only thing that makes summer at Vordingborg tolerable is the moose. Much has changed since Tycho found the moose in the bog-rosemary bushes. Now the moose is a large moose, a bull. It has thick velvet on its antlers; its head is the size of a firkin; it follows Tycho everywhere like a schoolgirl in love.

While Uncle Jørgen and King Frederick plot and strategize against the Swedes, Tycho and his moose go for long walks in the woods surrounding the castle. Sometimes they walk as far as the ocean. Even on the beach the air still smells of pine trees. There are white flowers on the dogwoods. A warm breeze blows from the east.

As they walk along the beach, Tycho talks loudly over the waves. He tells the moose about his plans for the universe. He wants to make his own ephemeris, but he needs a larger allowance. He needs better instruments, a radius that's large enough to measure the angles between the stars.

Normally attentive, the moose gazes distractedly down the beach, its ears turned toward some faraway sound.

Tycho hears it too.

Down the beach there's someone, many people, calling for help.

Tycho and his moose hurry toward the noise.

They round the bend and see a party of bathers.

The livery is King Frederick's: carmine on white.

Everyone is on the shore except for the king.

Tycho sees him in the water, caught in a riptide, drifting out to sea. He sees Uncle Jørgen sprinting into the ocean.

Tycho follows.

Moose gallops in as well.

But Tycho is a poor swimmer. He's unable to swim past the wave line. The surf pushes him back to the beach.

Uncle Jørgen reaches King Frederick but also gets caught in the riptide. Both men cling to each other, recede toward the horizon, drift away.

Steady as a boat, the moose paddles through the waves and reaches Uncle Jørgen and King Frederick. The men drape themselves over the moose's body and are transported back to shore.

8. DEARTH

That night the king orders a feast at the castle. There are torches, buglers, attendants in white gloves. Oxen, calves, and muffed cocks are slaughtered for the guests.

When dinner is served, the moose sits at the head of the table next to King Frederick. The moose doesn't sit, of course; it stands. Eats a plate of spinach and summer greens.

After the feast, King Frederick lifts his goblet and toasts Uncle Jørgen and the hero moose. He gives them both medals and makes a speech. He talks about the majestic though unpredictable and deadly nature of the sea. "Like a Dane," he says. "Like my mother," he says.

Everyone but the old queen laughs.

At the end of the ceremony, Uncle Jørgen, pale-looking, gold medal bright around his neck, excuses himself. He complains about a chill.

He pats the moose on its head.

Says goodnight to King Frederick.

Goodnight to Aunt Inger.

Goodnight to Tycho.

A week later, Uncle Jørgen dies.

9. THE END

End of the longest summer.

Tycho packs away his belongings. He fills his trunks with books, clothing, the new ephemerides that he bought with Uncle Jørgen's inheritance. He loads it all onto a coach and says goodbye to Aunt Inger.

Aunt Inger, who is still wearing black.

Tycho says goodbye to King Frederick.

Goodbye to all the servants.

Goodbye.

But from Vordingborg, he doesn't return to school in Copenhagen. He doesn't see the point. Why should he pretend to study the law if Uncle Jørgen isn't alive to care? Why spend all of his time bent over books, reading about the universe, when all he really needs to do is look up?

Instead, Tycho and his moose travel to northern Denmark, to Knudstrup Castle, one of his real parents' homes.

Knudstrup is isolated from everything. Its village has only two dozen cottages, five grain mills, and farmland that's as flat and expansive as the sky above.

The castle is so far north that during the summer, the sun barely sets. During the winter, white stars fill the daytime sky.

Tycho and his moose spend that autumn wandering through endless yellow fields of wheat and rapeseed. Tycho tells the moose that he misses Uncle Jørgen. He misses things that he didn't expect to miss about him. The sound of his uncle's laughter, the particular roughness of his beard.

Throughout the fall, Aunt Inger sends Tycho letters. She tells him how empty Vordingborg is without him. She misses the moose.

But instead of *moose*, Aunt Inger keeps calling the animal an *elk*. A common elk, as if there's anything common about it.

Tycho tosses her letters in the fire. At night there's no sound in the castle except for wood and paper burning, no sound at all except for Tycho and the moose's footsteps echoing off limestone as they pace outside on the castle's parapets, gazing at the sky.

There's the nebular spray of stars above them.

Warm lamplight from the village below.

Tycho presses the radius to his cheekbone. He lines up Jupiter in the first sight and finds Saturn with the second. He measures the angle, checks it against Ptolemy's measurement, and scowls.

According to Ptolemy's *Almagest*, the planets should be moving toward a conjunction, signaling expansion, social interaction, and material well-being.

But if Tycho's measurements are correct, the planets are actually moving away from each, approaching their square.

Bad energy, problems, frustration.

"All wrong," says Tycho. "Everything is wrong," he says.

The moose blinks open its eyes. A cold breeze rattles through the ephemeris. The moose yawns.

Tycho shoves his radius back into its case.

He walks down to the village.

The tavern.

Beer.

10. ASTRAL LOVE

Winter comes to Knudstrup.

Heavy clouds settle in and blank out the sky.

Tycho and the moose spend much of their time alone in the castle. Sometimes Tycho reads books in front of the fire. He reads astronomy books, astrology books, chivalric romances: *Robert the Devil, Amadis of Gaul, Havelok the Dane.*

But most of the time he doesn't read.

He drinks.

To pass the time.

Tycho sits in front of the fire, empty wine glass between his knees, and a journal open on his lap. On each page of the journal are sky measurements that he'd made during the previous summer and fall. There are coordinates for the traveling planets, lists of all the fixed objects in the ethereal sphere.

One at a time, Tycho rips out the pages and throws them into the fire. He rips out a sketch of Virgo and crushes it. But before he can toss it in the fire, he's interrupted by a knock at the door.

Tycho looks at the moose.

The moose looks back at Tycho. If a moose can shrug then that's what it does.

Shrugs.

There's another knock, and Tycho stumbles out of his chair. He knocks over an empty wine bottle on his way to open the door.

Behind the door is a gust of wind and a girl. The girl's eyes are deep and blue as the firmament; her hair is wheat.

She tells Tycho that she's there to deliver the firewood. She apologizes that the delivery is late. "My father," she says. "Sick," she says.

Tycho squints beyond her out the door. There are snowflakes in the moonlight, a horse attached to a cart. Tycho tells the girl to wait inside while he unloads the firewood. After he's finished, he offers her redcurrant wine.

The girl tells Tycho that her name is Kirsten Jørgensdatter; she's fourteen years old and lives in the village with her father. But Tycho already knows all this. He's seen her in church. He likes the way she wears her laced collars and cuffs, the way she braids her fingers when she prays. Her pale moon-shaped face.

He asks about her father, Jørgen Hansen, and she tells Tycho that he has a fever.

Tycho raises his glass and watches the fire through it, the smoke and logs rinsed red by the wine. He tells her that he once had an uncle named Jørgen. Then he tips back his glass and drains it, drinking to her Jørgen's health.

By the time they've finished the bottle, the fire has burned down to its embers. The moose leans against the wall, snoring.

Kirsten yawns and says that she should be going. She says that she shouldn't have left her father at home for so long.

Outside the castle, clouds swirl above them. The world is silent, a held breath.

Kirsten pulls up her hood and touches Tycho's hand. She thanks him and tells him that she had a nice night.

After she's gone, Tycho remains in the courtyard. There's the warm tingle on his hand where her hand touched his. The wall of clouds has split and for the first time all winter the stars are showing.

Venus in ascension.

Naked sky.

11. IN RUT

Tycho and Kirsten continue to make love all winter.

But it's love without kissing, love without hugging or handholding, love between a nobleman and a peasant girl. Chaste, forbidden, sixteenth-century love.

Even after her father has recovered, Kirsten delivers wood to Tycho's castle. They drink mulberry wine and Kirsten listens to Tycho talk about the universe. He tells her that the planets and the stars are forever isolated from one another, that they're locked in separate crystalline spheres.

He tells her that that's what their love is. He is a planet, and she is a star. Who could understand it?

No one, says Tycho. Not Otte Brahe, not Beate Bille, not Aunt Inger, not Jørgen Hansen, not Aristotle or Ptolemy.

Tycho tells Kirsten that the universe has an order to it. He tells her that their love breaks every law.

Then in March comes news that seems to affirm this.

Tycho receives a letter from Germany, from the University of Rostock, three hundred kilometers south of Kirsten. He's been accepted to study with the great astronomer Heinrich Brucaeus.

Brucaeus's *De motu primo libri tres* is one of Tycho's favorites.

There was no one he wanted to study with more.

12. THE HEAVENS PROVIDE

Tycho consults all of his books. He rereads the *Almagest*, the *Tetrabiblos*, the *Handy Tables*, the *Metaphysics*. Should he choose love or the university? Kirsten or the stars?

In a rare concurrence, the books all say the same thing. They agree that when Jupiter is in Sagittarius, the heavens signify optimism about the future and foreign travel. But in late-spring, when the king of planets is traveling between Sagittarius and Aries, the stars also signal innovation, new ventures, and expansion.

Tycho's decision is not to make a decision. The books seem to tell him that he doesn't need to choose between one love and the other. Because

Jupiter is traveling, he can go to Germany and expand his family. He's allowed to innovate; the old laws need not apply.

Tycho marries Kirsten a month before school starts. He hires a chaplain from Gothenburg, who performs the ceremony in the castle's chapel. It's not a *proper* marriage, not exactly; rather, it's a morganatic marriage. Marriage without dowry, without verbum, without Jørgen Hansen's consent. It's the only kind of marriage that the state will allow between a nobleman and a peasant. When Tycho dies, Kirsten won't be able to inherit his property. Her children won't be recognized as his heirs.

Still it's a love marriage. After Tycho says "I do" and Kirsten says "I do," he carries his bride up to their bedroom. Kirsten's gown trails on the steps behind them. Tycho smells the bundles of rosemary she's tied to her sleeves.

In the bedroom, Tycho unties her corset. He lifts her dress.

There's starry whiteness.

A fourteen-year-old's chest.

13. MY MOON, MY MAN

Tycho leaves for Rostock the next day.

He kisses his bride without waking her, pushes her hair behind her ears, and leaves an envelope next to her head.

Next, Tycho says goodbye to his moose. He strokes the moose's antlers and feeds it redcurrants. He tells the moose to mind Kirsten while he's gone.

Moose bugles sadly.

Then Tycho rides a horse to Gothenburg. He boards a boat and sails to Copenhagen. He boards another boat and sails away.

Back at Knudstrup, Kirsten wakes up and hears the moose bugling in the courtyard. She finds the envelope, opens it, and reads the poem that Tycho's written for her.

She rereads the part about how when they look at the stars at night they'll be looking at the same stars and so will always be together.

We live so far apart, and yet the beams

of radiant Olympus join our eyes at last.

She stands at the window and searches the sky for some object to fix her eyes upon. She finds the white crescent of the moon hanging above the horizon and stares at it.

She wonders what good it is being married to Tycho if he could just as happily be married to moonbeams instead.

14. THE FAMOUS STORY OF TYCHO'S NOSE

At last the boat arrives at Rostock. Tycho watches the city's skyline appear on the horizon. As it draws closer, the roofs, like sharp teeth, chew into the sky.

Above the skyline is the vestige of last night's moon. He traces its crescent with his eyes and imagines Kirsten doing the same.

When the boat finally docks, Tycho hires a coach to drive him to Brucaeus's castle, where Brucaeus is throwing a feast for his newest student. At the feast there's eel, olla podrida, and half a kid.

Tycho is introduced to another Danish student who's come to the university to learn from the great astronomer. His name is Manderup Parsbjerg; he has hair like a storm cloud and eyes that match.

Tycho and Parsbjerg sit across from each other at the feast table. They talk about the universe. "What about Copernicus?" asks Parsbjerg.

"Please," says Tycho. He leans across the table and pours Parsbjerg more wine. Tycho says that Copernicus may have had some good ideas, but that he really couldn't believe the theory that the Earth revolves around the sun.

Tycho tops off his wine. He watches it dribble over the top of his cup. "And what about the crystalline spheres?" he says. He asks what about the birds? What about the clouds? He asks Parsbjerg to explain to him how humans and other animals could stand on an Earth that's spinning through the universe like a top.

He pours himself more wine.

"I'll tell you what I think," says Tycho.

Tycho tells Parsbjerg that he thinks that the sun rotates around the Earth and that everything else rotates around the sun. He places his cup in the center of the table and tells Parsbjerg that the cup is the Earth. Then he sets the wine bottle next to it. The wine bottle is the sun.

Tycho pushes the wine bottle around the cup.

Then he takes Parsbjerg's cup and places it next to the wine bottle. The cup, he says, is everything else.

Tycho pushes the wine bottle around his cup and Parsbjerg's cup around the wine bottle. He tells Parsbjerg that his model of the universe is the only one that makes complete mathematical sense. Soon, he says, it will explain all of the cosmic mysteries. Parallax, retrograde motion, planetary drift.

"The mechanics of the universe explained," he says. He pounds the table to emphasize his point. His cup, Parsbjerg's cup, and the wine bottle all tumble over. A tide of red wine crashes into Parsbjerg's lap.

When Parsbjerg returns to the table, he removes his gloves, leans forward, and slaps Tycho's cheek.

"A duel," he says. He slaps the other cheek. "The harbor," he says.

15. THE FAMOUS STORY, CONTINUED

Dark rain hisses down on the cobblestones. There are seagulls asleep in the water, the swaying outlines of ships.

Parsbjerg drinks wine straight from the bottle. "Ready?" he says.

Tycho nods.

The two men touch swords. Then Parsbjerg cuts the nose off Tycho's face.

He swings his sword and smashes it through skin and cartilage. The sword slices a chunk off the bridge and cleaves through the entire tip.

Tycho's nose falls to the ground. His sword clatters down next to it.

Tycho's not far behind.

16. UNCLE JØRGEN

—stupidest thing.

Tycho groans. He opens his eyes and sees that he's still on the boat, that he's still sailing back home to Knudstrup. The ghost of Uncle Jørgen is still hovering above his bed.

Tycho groans again.

Beyond stupid, says the ghost. What were you thinking? he says. You've always been a horrible duelist. Could never tell pommel from tip.

The ghost tugs on his beard.

Booby, he says.

Blockhead.

Tycho squeezes his eyes closed. He feels the boat plunge underneath him and smells the dung-smelling poultice covering his face.

Clodpole, says the ghost.

Tycho's physician enters the cabin, and the ghost blinks out of existence. The physician checks Tycho's wound and replaces his poultice with a new one. He feeds Tycho a spoonful of camphor and ground elk hoof.

After the physician leaves, the ghost comes back.

Dunderhead, says the ghost.

Idiot.

Beef for brains.

17. KNUDSTRUP REVISITED

Moron.

Wretch.

The ghost floats at the foot of Tycho's bed. Outside the sun is rising above the wheat fields. Orange light creeps into the room.

Tycho covers his ears. "You're not here," he says.

No, says the ghost. Your nose is the only thing that's not here.

There's a knock on the door, and the ghost drifts toward it. He tells Tycho to open the door. He tells Tycho to let Kirsten in. So she can finally see what you've done to your face, he says.

Since Tycho's returned to Knudstrup, he hasn't seen Kirsten. Except for his physician, he hasn't seen anyone at all. He won't even look at himself in a mirror. He just probes the wound with his fingers, feeling the strange new flatness of his face.

Kirsten knocks again.

The ghost begins phasing through the door, passing in and out. Coward, says the ghost.

Chicken liver.

"Go away," says Tycho. "Leave me alone," he says.

Outside, Kirsten sets the tray of food on the floor and collects the old one. It's still full of Tycho's favorite things: smoked ox tongue, dogfish, Corbeil peaches. Tycho's barely taken a bite. After she delivers the tray to the kitchen, she tells Tycho's visitors that his condition hasn't changed.

Aunt Inger, Otte Brahe, Beate Bille, even King Frederick. They've all come to the castle to see Tycho. But Tycho won't see any of them. He's told Kirsten to turn them all away.

"I'm a monster," he yelled through the door, when Kirsten told him that the king had arrived. "I'll never see a living person again," he said.

The ghost agreed.

Worse than a monster, said the ghost, because even a monster has a nose.

18. THE MOOSE

Kirsten tells the king that Tycho won't see him.

"A shame," says the king. He tells Kirsten that he's already contacted his best surgeon. Tycho's not the first person to have lost his nose in a duel. He tells her to tell Tycho that there are things the surgeon can do.

On his way out, the king stops by the stables to visit the moose. It's been more than two years since he's seen the animal that saved his life. He has to squint into the shadows to find it. The moose is standing deep in the barn, beneath the hayloft. It's mangy, gaunt, and surrounded by flies.

The king extends an apple and the moose steps forward.

Moose grunts and bares its teeth.

The king drops the apple. He recalls the once majestic animal, how it pushed through the waves like a zephyr. It was the finest moose in all of Denmark.

Now it's this.

19. MORE OF THE SAME

Time passes.

How much? For Tycho it doesn't matter. It could be a week; it could be a month. Tycho doesn't leave his bedroom. He drinks until unconscious, wakes up, and pours himself another cup.

Outside his window, he watches Kirsten and her father working in the garden. They've planted tulips, hyacinths, and tomato plants. The sky is big and orange above them. There are towering cumulous clouds.

Tycho checks his wine bottle. Is it chardonnay? Chablis? Since the accident, everything tastes different. All of the flavors are muted, more diffuse.

The ghost hovers next to him. Accident, says the ghost. Give me a break, the ghost says. He asks Tycho if his decision to duel Parsbjerg was an accident. Was it an accident when he decided to draw his sword?

Tycho tips the rest of the wine into his cup. He sees Kirsten looking up at his window. She smiles and waves.

In his hurry to close the curtains, Tycho knocks over his cup. Wine spreads across his table. It soaks through his ephemerides, his astronomy books and notebooks, everything that Tycho has been checking and double-checking to see which of the universe's signs he must have misread. Does it matter that Kirsten is a Virgo? What do the *Handy Tables* say about marrying in May?

Wine drips into Tycho's lap.

Look at you, says the ghost. How could you hope to correct the universe? The ghost asks Tycho how he could even hope to correct his life.

For Tycho the ghost has a point. A father who's not a father. A wife who's not a wife. A nose that's not a nose. A moose that's not a moose. How do you correct something like that?

20. THE TYCHONIC SYSTEM

A day or so passes and the king's surgeon arrives to fix Tycho's nose. He offers to make Tycho a prosthetic. In exchange, the king wants Tycho's moose. The king writes in a letter that he wants to honor the noble animal. He has a spot for it in his stables. He feels that he owes much to the moose and that he hasn't given it enough. In the letter, the king says that he wouldn't be so presumptuous as to give Tycho counsel, but he confides that even a king knows what it's like to experience loss. He urges Tycho to take care of Kirsten. He reminds Tycho that, in many ways, she's all that he has.

And even Tycho is able to understand the king's implication: That Kirsten is all that he has *left*. That even she won't continue forever to suffer his neglect.

But instead of leaving his room and joining her in the garden to plant tulips, Tycho remains in his chair.

After the surgeon measures him for his prosthetic nose, he pours himself another glass of wine, ignores the ghost, and strokes his past.

For Tycho the past is his moose: the heroic moose, the compassionate moose, the moose that slept by the fire and let itself be decorated with bows. On the day the moose rescued King Frederick, Tycho was regaling the moose once again with stories of the eclipse. While they walked beneath the evergreens, Tycho was telling the moose about the blackness of the moon's umbra, about how the moon had overpowered the sun.

He told the moose that during the eclipse the stars shined with full intensity and that even the birds refused to take flight.

He told the moose about how he gazed up at the sky as the moon sliced across the face of the sun and turned day into night, proving to everyone who saw it that everything was reversible and that nothing was fixed.

Then he recalled how the moon continued on its trajectory, sliding past the sun. The stars disappeared, the sunlight returned, and the birds took flight again, the reversal reversed.

Their wings clapped as they lifted off and drifted away.

THE FOURTH MAN

It means nothing to me. I have no opinion about it, and I don't care.
—Pablo Picasso on news of the first moon landing,
quoted in the *New York Times*, July 21, 1969

#1

When the first man came back from the moon, everyone in America threw him a parade. There were forty-two parades in total. All of the women wanted to have his babies. All of the men wanted to shake his hand.

#2

The second man sat in the backs of red convertibles with the first man. They wore gold medals around their necks and went from parade to parade smiling and wiping confetti from their hair.

#3

Four months later, when the third man stepped out of his shuttle he was lifted onto the shoulders of his colleagues. NASA rocket scientists who had never carried anything heavier than decimal points lifted him above their heads and carried him into decontamination. When he got out, Tom Wolfe wrote a book about him. He never paid for a beer again.

#4

When the fourth man emerged from the spaceship, he was greeted by no one. He stood at the top of the metal staircase and watched the NASA rocket scientists carry the third man away. He unclasped his helmet and stepped aside for the NASA janitors who were already pushing their buckets into the rocket, eager to clean up the mess that he and the third man had made while in space.

PATTERNS

But it was always like this for the fourth man. Even when he was a child, he finished second to the mess. The fourth man's father worked for the Army Corps of Engineers and every year moved his family around the country so that he could build dams and prevent flooding.

Every year the fourth man lived near a river that

- had flooded
- was flooding
- was about to flood

FLOODS

In 1936, the fourth man's father moved the family to Fort Worth, Texas. That year the fourth man was four and the Brazos River crested at fifty-six feet. While his father smoked cigarettes and cursed his dam, and his mother filled sandbags, the fourth man raced toy boats in the floodwater that submerged his backyard. The first boat tipped over in an eddy, but the second sailed out of the yard and into the cow pastures. Even now the fourth man could remember how smoothly its white sails ducked underneath the split-rail fence and receded toward the horizon and disappeared.

NEW WORLD

The picture on the fourth man's Apollo Mission flight patch was of a boat sailing across the face of the moon. The boat had full white sails, dragged a trail of fire, and was modeled after Columbus's Pinta. Though the Pinta was not the first boat to reach the New World it was widely thought to be Columbus's favorite.

OLD WORLD

After his lunar module had touched down on the moon's surface, the fourth man prepared to read his statement. He was especially proud that he'd managed to work in the words that Columbus himself had inscribed on the bows of all his ships: "Following the light of the sun we left the Old World behind." But once the contact light flashed blue and the module settled into the dirt, the third man flipped the switch on the radio and casually uttered the words that all of the TV stations would choose to replay. "Man," said the third man, "that might have been a small one for Neil, but it was a long one for me."

SELFLESSNESS

When the US entered World War II, the fourth man's father enlisted to join the Army Air Corps. The newspapers were full of pictures of fighter pilots flying, fighting, and smiling overseas. But when the fourth man's father went to the recruiting station he learned that at thirty-five he was already too old to become a fighter pilot. He had to join the infantry instead. The fourth man's father spent the next five years in Europe, boots in the dirt, fighting the war.

HINDSIGHT

Was this the reason why the fourth man had become a pilot? Because his father could not? People sometimes asked him this. When they did the fourth man would laugh and tell them that there was nothing competitive about his relationship with his father. He'd say that he'd always loved airplanes and anything to do with flying. Even as a child he'd loved Buck Rogers, *Twelve O'Clock High*, bald eagles, and kites. He hadn't *become* a pilot, he'd say. He'd *been* a pilot all his life.

SACRIFICE

On the day the fourth man's father drove away to basic training, the fourth man stood at the top of the driveway and waved after his father's Chevy Cruiser. A steady wind pushed the smell of grass across the plains and the fourth man continued waving long after the black car's taillights were out of sight.

SACRIFICE

For five years there was no Little League, no marching band, no touch football, no family vacations to Holiday Beach. But it wasn't just like this for the fourth man; everyone else's father was *also* fighting the war.

WHAT WE LEARNED

During the war the fourth man's mother opened a grocery store. Within a year she'd expanded from one store to two. By the end of the war she owned four grocery stores and an ice cream shop. When the fourth man's father came home, he could have quit his job and worked for her.

HARD WORK

Is a quality that's not emphasized enough in public schools. For example, in elementary and high school the fourth man's favorite subject had always been math. He liked math because it was relatively straightforward; if you knew the equations you could solve the problems. Still his grades were never any better than Bs and Cs. It wasn't until he went to college and joined the NROTC that he learned that if he worked harder he could do better. It was then that he had 4:00 AM wake up calls, seven-mile runs, pushups, sit ups, and the drill sergeant's hot breath in his face. He could still recall the warm swell of pride he felt when he earned his first A minus in calculus, when he ran his first six-minute mile, when the drill sergeant told him that he'd graduated from maggot to scum.

#5

They say that the fifth man was the unlucky one because he never got to actually set foot on the moon. But he was the one who said, "Houston, we've had a problem." After that, Tom Hanks played him in the movie of his life. It was nominated for nine Academy Awards and won two.

THE RUSSIANS

Before Gagarin, the Russians launched fifty-seven dogs into space. The first and most famous dog to achieve full orbit was Laika who died seven hours into the mission from stress and overheating. Next, though less well-known, were Belka and Strelka, who went up together, spent a full day in orbit, and returned to Earth alive. What's not often mentioned is that Belka and Strelka didn't go up alone. They were accompanied by one gray rabbit, two white rats, and forty-two mice all of which *also* returned to Earth alive.

RECOGNITION

Imagine throwing a dart and hitting a perfect bull's-eye. Now imagine that the dart weighs five tons and the bull's-eye is sixty miles away. Essentially that's what the fourth man had been asked to do. His job was to pilot the lunar module off the surface of the moon and reconnect it with the mothership that was orbiting above, traveling at an average land speed of 3,500 mph. It was a once-in-a-lifetime shot and is made no less impressive by the fact that the fourth man had spent six years practicing for it. Imagine what it takes to spend six years preparing for just one perfect moment.

#6

Was played by Kevin Bacon in the fifth man's movie. After his NASA career, the sixth man was elected to Congress by a landslide. When he died they named a middle school after him in Colorado. He has a big statue in Washington, DC.

DAMS

One common misconception about the fourth man's father is that he only built dams. But if you go out to Possum Kingdom or Somerville or any of the other dozen new lakes and recreation areas that have sprung up along the Brazos River since the 1940s you can see for yourself that dams are only half the father's story. He built *reservoirs*.

MONUMENTS

After the war, the fourth man's father traveled to places like Arkansas, Louisiana, and Tennessee to build new dams. He'd be gone for months at a time, and, for a long time, the fourth man thought that his father was ignoring him. But later, as an adult, he realized that he could drive to almost any reservoir in the four-state area, sit in the shadow of its dam, look up at the two hundred vertical feet of concrete, and know that his father had had a hand in building it. In another one or two hundred years his father's dams would still be there. How many other sons could claim a legacy like that?

WHAT WE LEARNED

In terms of pure scientific discovery, some people say that we didn't learn enough to justify the tremendous costs of multiple return trips to the moon. But these are the kinds of people who don't understand what George Mallory meant when he said, "Because it's there." What we learned is that we were able to put twelve Americans on the moon and send more than double that number into lunar orbit. There's no other nation in history that has done anything close. Columbus only sailed to the New World four times. Magellan only circumnavigated the globe once.

THE PRESIDENT

"This is the greatest week in the history of the world since the Creation" is what the president said after the first and second man came back from the moon. When the fifth and sixth man returned he hosted a dinner for them, and spoke of their "special qualities" and "extraordinary concert of skills." What would the president have said about the fourth man if the two had ever met? This is something that the fourth man would also like to know.

PRIDE

Besides walking on the moon, the fourth man's next proudest moment was earning his first pair of Naval aviator wings. In 1955, he'd spent a year in Beeville practicing takeoffs and landings, takeoffs and landings, until the time came for the graduation ceremony in June. By then his father was in Tennessee, on the Tennessee River, building what would become the Boone Dam. The fourth man could still remember how hot he'd been in his Navy whites, the shadeless bleachers with the one empty seat that he'd reserved for his father, the way his mother's hands shook when she pinned the bronze wings to his chest.

REGRETS

The fourth man believed in living a life without them. There's no point dwelling on the past when what really matters is always what's happening next. Still if he could go back and change one thing, he'd have liked it if his father had been alive to see him walk on the moon.

POSITIVE MENTAL ATTITUDE

When Vincent van Gogh painted "Starry Night," no one said that it was one of the best paintings ever painted. It took people years to recognize and appreciate the genius of what he'd done. The same is true for many of history's famous people. The *New York Times* misspelled Herman Melville's name in his obituary. It took two hundred years for Copernicus's theory to be confirmed. So was the fourth man worried that he wasn't immediately as well-known as some of the other men who'd walked on the moon? He'd prefer to let history be the judge of who is remembered and who is not.

#7

The seventh man to fly to the moon was also the second man to have flown in space after Gagarin. Even before he planted the American flag in lunar soil, everyone already knew who he was.

#8

The eighth man is the astronaut who NASA wishes everyone would forget. He was the first man to throw a javelin on the moon and the only astronaut to state publically and often his belief in extraterrestrials. After NASA, the eighth man founded the Institute of Noetic Studies, which, according to its literature, "conducts and supports research into areas that more mainstream scientists do not entertain." Think aliens; think remote healing; think ESP.

PRESENCE

Some astronauts say that they felt God's presence on the moon, but it wasn't quite like that for the fourth man. When he floated down to the surface and bounded from crater to desolate crater, he too felt as if someone else was there bounding along with him, though it wasn't God. How to explain it except to say that there's a special bond that connects father and son?

REMEMBER

To say that the fourth man's father spent much of his time away from his family building dams is not to suggest that he was totally absent. Some of the fourth man's best memories are the ones of his father coming home.

HOMECOMING

In 1961, the fourth man was working on ejection seats in Jacksonville, Florida. There was an electrical malfunction that year which caused some of the seats to misfire. The seats wouldn't eject or, when they did, their parachutes wouldn't deploy. Good pilots died. This was also the year that the fourth man's father suffered a catastrophic heart attack while on a walk around the reservoir at Possum Kingdom. *Plunging* is how the fourth man would later describe the sensation of suddenly returning home. He didn't fly home, and he didn't hurry home. From the moment after he hung up the phone with his mother, he plunged.

RE-ENTRY

On their return trip from the moon, as their capsule plunged through the miles of upper atmosphere, the third man looked out the window, at the sky lighting up yellow and orange with flames around them, and tried to describe the feeling of endless descent. He said he'd never felt anything like it. Not so for the fourth man. He said that he'd felt it once before.

FLOODS

A flood is usually taken to mean a great flowing or overflowing of water, but it can also be used to express an outpouring of emotion, as in: a *flood* of tears.

MAGNIFICENT DESOLATION

What surprised the fourth man most about the moon was its complete barrenness. Sure he'd known from the experience of other astronauts that the surface of the moon was a wasteland. "Magnificent desolation," is how the second man described it. Others talked about the moon's essential grayness, its sand like ash. Still, how to comprehend such an empty landscape? As the fourth man walked across the moon's battered surface, the Earth glowed blue like an aquarium in the distance.

NEVER THE SAME

They say once you travel beyond the Earth's atmosphere you've been essentially changed. Gamma rays begin to bombard you at 328,000 feet. Bones and muscles lose density in the vacuum. Weightlessness often causes space-sickness with nausea and vomiting. When Gagarin returned from his first space flight, he complained of black dots dancing around the edge of his vision. He was stricken with headaches. Though he'd been a lifelong atheist, he had his daughter baptized almost as soon as he stepped off the plane.

#9

The ninth man smuggled more than three hundred commemorative stamps with him to the surface of the moon. When he returned he sold them to a German stamp dealer for a lot of money, which he used to establish a trust fund for the families of Apollo astronauts. Though

NASA let him keep the money, they made sure that he never flew a space mission again.

#10

Had a minor heart attack on the moon. When he came back, he founded the High Flight Ministries and dedicated the rest of his life to finding Noah's Ark. After several unsuccessful expeditions to Mount Ararat, he retired to Colorado Springs where he suffered his third major heart attack. He was the first man who walked on the moon to die.

#11

The eleventh man brought a framed picture of his family with him to the moon and left it on the surface under the American flag. They say that with a strong enough telescope you can still find the picture. You can still see the footprints of all the men who walked on the moon.

IMPRESSIONS

When the fourth man came back from the moon he enrolled himself in painting classes. At first he couldn't say why he was taking them except that he'd always liked beautiful things. His favorite airplanes to fly were always the sleekest and most beautiful. His favorite dam that his father built was the one with buttresses. He liked that while painting he could lay one color on top of another and increase the beauty of both. It was like mathematics, the way you can add two numbers to create a greater sum. The first painting he made that he ever thought successful was called *Hopes And Dreams* and showed a spaceship blasting off. At first, the picture didn't capture the grandeur of the actual event, so he painted a rainbow in the sky behind it. What the fourth man liked best about painting is that you could solve problems with colors.

#12

The twelfth man was the final man to walk on the moon. By then the national mood had changed. Even the fourth man didn't watch it on television. That night more people watched reruns of *Hawaii Five-O*. The fourth man had been up to the space station to do experiments with spiders, he'd trained with the Russians in Space City, he'd been made NASA's chief astronaut, and he was thinking of retiring so that he could paint full-time.

CELEBRATION

The fourth man's next successful painting was of two astronauts leaping off the surface of the moon, their hands meeting in high fives. The Earth is high in the sky above them and in the background there's a big billowing American flag. This never happened, of course; the moon missions were dangerous and the mood much too serious. But it's what should have happened, again and again.

INSPIRATION

One astronaut floating in space above another who's lying in repose on the surface of the moon. Both astronauts have their fingers extended toward each other in an imitation of Michelangelo's famous scene on the ceiling of the Sistine Chapel, the one where God gives Adam life.

TRUTH

It's true that the fourth man took his father's remains with him to the moon. The final thing he did before returning to the lunar module was scatter his father's ashes. He tossed the ashes and watched them mix with moon dust. In this sense, you could say that his father really was with him on the moon. You could also say that his father is still up there, that he's permanently 286,000 miles away.

REMEMBRANCE

A more somber painting than most of the others: a ghostly astronaut standing on the moon's surface. The astronaut's legs are transparent and fade until they become indistinguishable from the surface of the moon itself.

SEE YOU AGAIN

By the time the fourth man arrived at the emergency room, his father had passed away. The fourth man was told that his father held on longer than anyone had expected, that he insisted on seeing his son before saying his final goodbye. But this was just like the fourth man's father. He always insisted on saying a proper goodbye to everyone, because, he said, a proper goodbye always implied its corollary. Whenever the fourth man stood at the top of the driveway and waved goodbye to his father, his father would lean out the window of his Cruiser, honk the horn, and yell, "I'll see you again."

SELF-PORTRAIT

There are two astronauts on the moon tossing a football. One of the astronauts is the father and the other, obviously, is the son. In the picture, the son is holding the football and wants to toss it to the father who's running away from him, sprinting toward a crater. If you look closely, through the son's visor, you'll see that his mouth is open and that he's shouting something. If you could hear him, you'd hear that he's shouting. "Turn around," he says. "Look at me. I'm here. I'm here."

GOOD WITH WORDS

"Give me more," she says.

"More?" I say. My voice breaks a little, a whine. "But I don't have more. I've given you what I've given you. It's all I've got."

"I need more," she says. "Fifty thousand. Fifty thousand is the bare minimum. If you don't have fifty thousand you don't have anything at all."

"Nothing?" I say.

My publisher shakes her head. "Nothing. No book."

I jam my hands into my pockets and poke around. I've got some lint in there, a quarter and some pennies, my car keys, my wallet with my driver's license and a couple of credit cards, a screw that I'd found lying on my son's bookshelf. What had a screw been doing on his bookshelf? I don't know. But he's one year old and I thought I'd better put it in my pocket before he found it and put it in his mouth.

What I don't have is more words.

No conjunctions, no prepositions. Not even a common noun, cow. I certainly don't have any good words. Not a limpid, for example. My favorite word because it sounds so dirty, the opposite of what it means.

Not, of course, that I expected to find words in my pockets anyway. I'm not an idiot. Not really. But it's not like I have all these extra words in my head.

The waitress comes back with our check. My publisher signs for our coffee and omelettes. She sighs. "Look," she says. "Give me forty-five thousand. That's only five thousand more than you've already got."

But the words I already have, those forty thousand? Aren't they good words? Good enough? I mean I think they're okay. I chose them carefully, thought about them kind of hard, and put them into a deliberate order. I bet if you read them they'd do something to you. Make you feel something. Maybe you'd laugh a little or feel sort of sad. I bet you'd feel something at least half a dozen times. And six feelings from forty thousand words is actually pretty good alchemy. Ask anyone else who writes.

Not that anyone understands this. It's not just my publisher. My sister's like that too. She wants me to write something to say at her wedding, a speech. "I don't know about what," she says from Ohio on the phone to me here in California. "Something about love," she says. "How hard can it be? You're a writer. You're good with words."

I'm not that good with words, actually. My son has two words, maybe two and a half. He's got mama and papa and sometimes it sounds like he's saying hi. He's way better with his words than I am with mine. Each time he uses his words he makes me feel something. One hundred percent of the time.

"Tell me something about love," I say when it's just the two of us. My wife's at yoga and the dog is napping and we've played with all his toys and I don't want to turn on *Sesame Street*.

He says, "Mama."

"That's good," I say. "Wow you nailed it. Now tell me something else. Something funny, something that makes you laugh."

He says, "Papa."

I tickle him and kiss his head.

"Great," I say. "Now tell me what you want. What do you want more than anything in the world? Sky's the limit. Name it and it's yours."

He lifts his arms up for me to hold him.

He says, "Hi."

ACKNOWLEDGMENTS

No book is a solitary effort and so I must thank all of my brilliant friends and colleagues who helped me along the way. My thanks to Sean Bernard, Josh Bernstein, Stephan Clarke, Emily Fridlund, Alexis Landau, Lisa Locascio, Josie Sigler, Cody Todd, and most of all to Bonnie Nadzam, whose friendship and readership improved every one of these stories. To my teachers, Lee K. Abbott, Emily Anderson, Aimee Bender, T.C. Boyle, Michelle Herman, Dana Johnson, Erin McGraw, and Jim Shepard, for the heroic amount of time, faith, and effort they've given me over the years. To Kate Johnson, my agent, who has been a tireless champion of my work. To all of the editors who first published these stories in magazines and literary journals. To Alissa Nutting for awarding this book the Starcherone Prize. To Kate, Mark, and everyone at Red Hen.

Most of all, my thanks to my family: my grandparents, Michael and Lois Polk; my aunts and uncles; my parents, Jeanne and John Hurt; my sister, Emily Hurt; and my son, Ezra Hurt. Without your unconditional love, support, and optimism, none of these stories would exist.

Finally, I want to single out, praise, and celebrate Marielle Henault, my first, last, and best reader, whose faith in me exceeds reason, and who is the best person in my life. Thank you for every single day of our wonderful life together.

BIBLIOGRAPHY

The stories in this book were much improved by and so owe much to the following sources: Jenny Uglow's *The Lunar Men*; Maria Edgeworth's *Memoirs of Richard Lovell Edgeworth, Esq.*; Anna Seward's *Memoirs of the Life of Dr. Darwin*; Elaine Sciolino's "Magic Measured in a Pile of Salt"; Tom Vanderbilt's "Let the Robot Drive: The Autonomous Car of the Future Is Here"; Burkhard Bilger's "Auto Correct: Has the Self-Driving Car at Last Arrived?"; Joe Palca's "The Scientist Who Makes Stars On Earth"; Alec Wilkinson's *The Ice Balloon: S.A. Andree and the Heroic Age of Arctic Exploration*; Apsley Cherry-Garrard's *The Worst Journey in the World*; Anthony Brandt's *The Man Who Ate His Boots: The Tragic History of the Search for the Northwest Passage*; Chauncey Loomis's *Weird and Tragic Shores: The Story of Charles Francis Hall, Explorer*; Ken McGoogan's *Fatal Passage: The Story of John Rae, the Arctic Hero Time Forgot*; John Robert Christianson's *On Tycho's Island: Tycho Brahe, Science, and Culture in the Sixteenth Century*; Kitty Ferguson's *Tycho and Kepler: The Unlikely Partnership That Forever Changed Our Understanding of the Heavens*; Joshua and Anne-Lee Gilder's *Heavenly Intrigue: Johannes Kepler, Tycho Brahe, and the Murder Behind of One of History's Greatest Scientific Discoveries*; Andrew Chaikin's *A Man on the Moon*; Alan Bean's *My Life as an Astronaut*; and, of course, Wikipedia.

BIOGRAPHICAL NOTE

Bryan Hurt is the editor of *Watchlist: 32 Stories by Persons of Interest*. His stories and essays have appeared in *The American Reader*, *Guernica*, the *Kenyon Review*, the *Los Angeles Review of Books*, *TriQuarterly*, and many other publications. He is an assistant professor of English at Capital University in Columbus, Ohio, where he lives with his family.

CPSIA information can be obtained
at www.ICGtesting.com
Printed in the USA
BVHW08s1033070618
518428BV00002B/3/P